Confession

A Novel

PHILIP SCHULMAN, MD

FIRST PRINTING, March 2022.
Harry Markos, Director.

Paperback: ISBN 978-1-914926-76-1
eBook: ISBN 978-1-914926-77-8

Book design by: Ian Sharman

www.markosia.com

First Edition

Dedicated to my loving wife, Sherry, who has always supported me and provided invaluable editorial assistance for this work, and to my wonderful children, who are my joy and reason for being.

PROLOGUE

She walked the dark streets of Greenwich Village alone as she had done so often but tonight was different. It seemed hauntingly darker and more ominous. Thunder and lightning added to the eeriness. She had an especially hard day and wanted desperately to get home and see her daughter who was turning eleven today. The party that she had planned was going to be special. She had ordered her daughter's favorite meal from the Japanese restaurant in SOHO and a white cake with pink buttercream flowers and strawberry mouse filling. Her husband would be home shortly; everything was ready and waiting for the celebration. She turned onto Perry Street from Greenwich and continued forward toward their apartment on Perry Street.

Lightning and thunder struck again, which sent a shiver through her spine. She thought *why am I so unnerved tonight? I've completed this walk hundreds of times.* As she approached her building, he watched her as the tension built in his being. Placing her fingers around the doorknob, she felt a violent shove. A hand reached out for her and was followed by a blow to her head. He turned her around and she could see his face. She was startled to see a young man no more than sixteen or seventeen staring at her, with a malicious, callous almost sadistic look in his eyes. She struggled but he hit her again and she momentarily was stunned. He then dragged her into an alley way. She screamed and struggled, but knew it was to no avail in these empty dark streets. Fear, anxiety and an inevitable foreboding grew as he hit her again. She felt him raping her and felt her resistance ebb when the blade slashed across her neck. That was the last thing she remembered.

Hearing the screams and the struggle, a neighborhood passerby ran toward its genesis, but all he saw was a woman lying in the alleyway appearing dead with blood everywhere. He ran to an open convenience store and asked the owner to call the police.

"A woman was just killed on Perry Street. Call an ambulance and the cops, hurry."

He returned to the woman, inspected her for any signs of life, but there were none and stood there facing the alleyway while waiting for help to arrive.

Two policemen arrived on Perry Street, saw the witness, who was still waiting, getting more and more soaked in the persistent rainfall and walked over to him.

"Yes, my name is Detective Captree from the 6th precinct," said the cop.

"Ssshe's over there!" said the witness pointing to the alleyway with a wet shaking index digit.

Captree moved toward the body, lying face down. He turned her around, looked at her face and slumped to the ground next to her, his face growing pale, his eyes opening wide with a look of shock. Seeing Captree slump to the ground, his partner rushed over and asked, "Are you OK? What is it, what's the matter?"

Bending down, facing the victim, he realized what had caused Captree's distress. He stared again at the woman to confirm what he perceived at first glance. He realized that what he first saw was veritable and began sobbing, holding Captree in a tight embrace.

"I'm so, so sorry. My God. No."

Captree looked at his partner, cried and shouted a guttural, very loud, "My wife. My wife. Veronica, Veronica, No. No. What am I going to do?"

Captree slumped on top of his wife and cried in load, deep sobs. The witness stared at the woman, the detective and the blood and started retreating this mess. He began walking toward Greenwich Street.

"Hey, partner, Where the fuck do you think you're going?"

"Ah, Um. I called it in, I did my civic duty. I have to leave now."

"Oh yeah, just like that, huh? I guess you don't think we need to ask you anything and you're free to go," said the partner furiously.

"Guess again, buddy. I think you'll be coming with us to the precinct. I believe we have a few questions for you, seemingly the only eyewitness," he continued.

"Come on, guys. I don't know anything."

"Just wait here!" The partner picked Captree up and, said. "Ron, your apartment is right here. Go home and take care of Claudia. I'll take care of this shit."

Captree arose walked to the apartment building in a slow deliberate gait as if in a fog, looked again in the alleyway, screamed again, "No! No!" turned back and unlocked the front door and walked in.

PART ONE
BEAUMONT TO NEW YORK

Throw your dreams into space like a kite and you do not know what it will bring back, a new life, a new friend, a new love, a new country.

-Anais Nin

Chapter 1

Lying awake, tossing and turning, I kept thinking of the day to come. I had been having difficulty sleeping for the past week in anticipation of what was to transpire over the next few hours. I felt bewildered, apprehensive and anticipatory about my intent, but the force of the urge was insurmountable and could not be curtailed. I had to do this. Not gaining any benefit from just lying there, I bolted out of bed to prepare for the day. I showered, shaved my few bristles of beard and brushed my teeth. I stared at the mirror at my non-descript face and noted the blemishes, the longish hooked nose, the square chin and the shock of curly hair; the entire picture presenting an awkwardly handsome face. The eighteen plus years I had lived thus far had not yet positively impacted my skin, my physique or my senses but my mind and psyche had been formed and immersed in an uncontrollable urge. I only wished I could calculate and understand its derivation and genesis so that maybe I could stop it, but I couldn't understand it, nor could I control it, and, thus, I didn't think I could derail its eventuality. I continued to dress: white shirt, gray slacks, black shoes and finally the cap and gown.

Today was my high school graduation. To my surprise, I was picked to deliver the salutatorian address for the class of 2018 of Beaumont High School. It was still only 6a.m. so I had a few hours to review the speech, make last minute changes and "relax". *Could I really be calm, placid and tranquil today? I thought most likely not.* I went to the bedroom window and stared outside at the bucolic setting. The Massachusetts sunlight shone through the window as the green trees swayed in a gentle breeze. I appreciated this area and Beaumont specifically, the school and town. I had accomplished much here but graduation was to be my farewell. I was going to college in New York and would spend the summer there as an intern at "New", a literary magazine, with an emphasis on technology intended for young, impressionable readers, yet, sophisticated enough to understand the deeper meanings and themes of its content while at the same time illuminating advances in AI. This was truly a dream appointment for a loner with writing aspirations. I sat at my desk and reviewed my remarks:

My fellow graduates: Today marks a beginning, a new day to follow our dreams. We are no longer tied to our homes, our parents or to Beaumont. We are now free to pursue our goals. Many of us will be off to college and to other homes, towns and cities, but let us not forget Beaumont or what we have accomplished here and how this school facilitated our successes. We entered as wide-eyed freshman with little experience or accomplishments, and we leave as older teenagers gaining a modicum of experience, but with aspirations and hopefully, a bright future. I sincerely wish you all congratulations and future success. I hope you choose the right road when you are facing the inevitable fork. I sincerely hope your choice brings you happiness, and comfort. As I look out at you, I am struck, though, by the dichotomy of our class, surely a reflection of the variability and diversity of our town, with its many personalities, strengths and weaknesses. We are all unique with our quirks, personalities, ambitions and goals. To my surprise, I am standing in front of you in spite of my lack of social graces or camaraderie. My reticent and insular personality may have alienated you. You may even deem me the Holden Caulfield of Beaumont. If you do, I understand but I also want to tell you that I feel closer to you guys than ever before and believe me I think highly of you and appreciate your energy, work ethic and intelligence. You have all led the way for me. It is not that I don't aspire to more friends, it is somehow not in my personality or my singularity, but I can safely say that our class has inspired me to strive mature and grow. I hope you all understand and empathize.

As easily perceived, the world is very divided and threatened and we must be the leaders for our future to be secure. So, in spite of my introversion, I say please make the commitment to walk with me and prove that this generation is the great one.

Thank you.

I realized that this was inimitable for a salutatorian address, which is usually more generic and less personal and intimate. I stared at the paper and thought, were these private and personal thoughts going to elicit laughter, mocking and ridicule because no one seemed to understand me or like me? But then again, did I understand myself or better yet did I truly appreciate my own psyche and mental state? I wanted to make the speech real and personal but added the proverbial last paragraph about saving the world and being the next Great Generation to comply with the norm.

I walked out the door of my smallish bedroom, closing the door of the blue painted room, neatly appointed with a bed frame without a headboard, a desk strewn with papers and built-in bookshelves with copies of my favorite books: "Catcher in the Rye", "Catch 22", and "One Flew over the Cuckoo's Nest", my still to be returned text books, my journals and my collection of pens. I slowly walked to the kitchen and found my mother excitedly preparing breakfast while anticipating the day ahead. Her son was the salutatorian of Beaumont High, probably the quintessential small town high school with a national reputation for placing students in the best colleges and boasting national rankings at the top in standardized test score and high school rankings. As I approached her, I thought that her pride and love were genuine and real and yet I felt a deep regret and ambivalence about our relationship. She never attempted to stop her husband's incessant belligerence toward me, and she had displayed an inappropriate relationship with me, as well. She didn't know, nor would I ever tell her of the totality of his abuse. I kept it to myself and suffered through it. The anger against him and his malicious treatment of me was always a theme and focus of my daily life.

"Morning mom," I commented strolling into the room.

"Morning, dear Evan. How are you? Did you sleep well?"

"Sure mom," I replied lying again to her about my sleep habits.

My mother, Sandra Dicks was a petite woman of forty-one years. She was attentive to her two sons, my brother James and me but and a very affectionate, solicitous wife. She carefully minded her home, family and her uncaring abusive husband, Thomas Dicks, a tall handsome man of fifty-seven years. He had an athletic, muscular build that was now showing signs of losing its tone. His rugged mustachioed face displayed a smallish jaw, slightly down turned slanted eyes and graying curly hair. Thomas Dicks, an electrical engineer, provided well for his family, but somehow his quick temper and irrepressible anger negated all that was good about him. He mostly abused his sons, especially me but he also abused his loving devoted and neglected wife. Yet she remained dutiful, loyal and presumably faithful to him. She continuously turned a blind eye to his mistreatment of her sons as if hypnotized by her love and rapture. Both James and I remained taciturn and reticent. Although I usually received the brunt of his abuse, we both refused to unveil his true personality filled with acrimony.

"Hey, Mom, how are you. Is dad up yet? I suppose he will be joining us at the graduation," I queried her facetiously.

"Are you kidding? Of course, he's coming. He's your father or did that small fact skip your mind?" she replied assertively.

"Of course. Sorry, I was only kidding," I acknowledged with the faintest smile of indignation.

As I sat at the breakfast nook table, Mom served scrambled eggs, toast and fruit. I wasn't exactly hungry or in the mood for food but ate it nonetheless to please her. As I was finishing. my eggs, my younger brother strolled in as did my father not too far behind. We sat at the table silently as we had done during so many of our meals

together over the years. We were a quiet family
without much mealtime conversation. I excused
myself and walked back to my room to continue the
review of my speech. I sat at my desk looked at the
speech but all I could think about was the coming
event. I kept thinking about Emily O'Connell, the
valedictorian. She was a pleasant pretty girl, eighteen
years old and obviously very intelligent. We usually
exchanged salutations at church and, of course, in
class, but didn't otherwise, have a relationship. We
had pleasant conversations about school, the class
or other local events and issues, but never dated or
met socially. I did understand that she was one of
the most popular girls in school with a large social
circle. I had even heard that she was a bit "loose,"
which bothered me and my religious sensibilities.
But did I really have anything against her? I wasn't
jealous, perturbed by her success or specifically
angry with her. But the negative thoughts about
her never ceased or stopped. Those feelings were
constantly there. They probably were there for
some time but now I had to *act* on them. I pictured
Emily. She had a round pretty face framed by long
wavy blonde hair. Her round blue eyes commanded
attention and their sparkle defined her intelligence.
Whenever we spoke, she always seemed pleasant,
receptive and responsive. Yet, I kept thinking
about my deep feelings. Her effervescent, outgoing
personality was obviously diametrically opposed to
my own introversion. Maybe that defined my psyche

and my animosity. I could no longer tolerate these thoughts or their ramifications. Trying to dismiss them, I put my head on my desk and closed my eyes. I rested and tried to empty my brain.

At 11am, we left for the Beaumont High School campus. It was set up with rows of seats, and flowers lining the main aisle for the graduation procession. The dais housed seats for the administration, the district heads, the valedictorian and the salutatorian. The graduation had all the pomp and circumstance of an Ivy League university. The class slowly strolled down the central aisle to the recorded music of the "Graduation Processional March" by Chris V. Sibayar. When they reached their rows, each graduate chose their own seat and waited as Emily and I climbed the stage to the dais. We all stood and waited for the march to end, and we sat in unison. The program was of moderate length highlighted by the speeches of the principal, the district head and an assortment of teachers. This was followed by the announcement of the awards, which were dominated by Emily O'Connor. She won most of the major awards including the English and literature awards along with a number of scholarships. I won a physics and creative writing award, which pleased my dad for one of the few times I could remember. After I completed my speech to mild applause while noting some hesitancy and ambiguity of the audience and the suspected snickering at my comments, I returned to my seat to listen to Emily.

She spoke eloquently of her times at Beaumont High, her friends and of the class she was leading. She also spoke of her aspirations, goals and wishes for the class, and herself and the future. Emily clearly had stage presence and commanded attention. But I was in my own world, nearly completely immersed in my own feelings and thoughts. She continued for approximately twenty minutes and then retook her seat. The ceremonial dispensing of the diplomas completed the program and as the class stood to flip their hats, I sat and watched not moving or standing. I sat and sat and waited for the completion of the ceremony. It was getting close to the time. I waited. A small shutter of excitement traversed my bones. My palms were moist, and my hands trembled. The excitement rose in my being as I felt I would soon realize my release.

That night I was invited to the post-graduation party at Emily's house. All hundred and three graduates were invited so I wasn't surprised that I was included. Her house, a majestic five thousand square foot home on two acres backing a green preserve, was clearly the archetypal house in Beaumont. Her father was a cardio-thoracic surgeon at Massachusetts General Hospital, the famous *MGH* of Boston, which was approximately thirty miles southeast of Beaumont. They obviously were the wealthiest or one of the wealthiest families in Beaumont. Beaumont was a diverse town of fifty thousand people or so. The population was composed of mostly Christians but did include a sizable Jewish population. The median income was considered one of the highest in the state. Nonetheless, there was also a sizable population of people of color. The non-white population did associate with the white population, in a friendly congenial manner but without real social interaction. This was obviously evident at Emily's party where the twenty graduates of color did not attend. The party was the usual teen get together with loud music, animated conversations and clandestine liquor and drug use. However, I mostly sat alone in my dreams and feelings. I was about ready to leave when Emily approached me.

"Hi, Ev. Are you enjoying my party?"

"Yeah. It's fun."

"I hear you're going to New York next week?" she politely asked trying to make conversation.

"I am. I have an internship at "New" and I'll be staying at the Columbia dorm," I replied.

"Wow so mature and grown up and ready to fend for yourself. Impressive!"

"Thanks," I replied.

"Hey, by the way, would you like to dance?" she asked suggestively.

I was startled by this question and surprised by her suggestion and her body language. But I answered affirmatively so we strolled to the center of the vast backyard by the pool and came together in an embrace while beginning to slowly sway to "All of Me" by John

Legend. She inched very close to me rubbing her breasts against my chest and her pelvis against my hips. What the fuck was she doing? I thought she was a good Christian girl. This was inappropriate and really disturbed and discomforted me. I moved away and noted the disbelief, surprise and amazement in her reaction. *I guess no one ever rejected you before. Well good for you, you little slut.* We separated when the song ended.

"I'm sorry Emily. You kind of surprised and caught me off guard. I didn't mean to back off or not to respond," I lied. "Matter of fact, I kind of enjoyed it and would like to continue. Would you like to meet sometime?" I suggested initiating my plans.

Amazed at my response she replied, "Wow, Cool. That would be great, when?"

"Let's meet tomorrow night. But we probably should keep our meeting quiet. I don't think you'd want to ruin your reputation, right?" I said pathetically but with full honesty.

"You're crazy. I find you interesting and surely attractive," she answered.

"Thanks, but doesn't everyone consider me a creep and weird."

"I don't care," she said emphatically.

"Thanks, but let's keep things quiet for a while anyway, OK?"

"Sure."

We agreed to meet the next day at the Beaumont Arboretum. As the sun set, the dusk cast a pink hue over the tress, plants and flowers of the beautiful park. I sat on a bench near the entrance and waited. Waiting for her to arrive, I felt my built-up adrenalin needing release. At 8:05 she strolled in with a confident, radiant air about her. She sat next to me and put her smallish, dainty beautiful hand with the long fingers and the perfectly blue painted nails on my knee.

"Hey. So good to see you," she said in a whisper both deep and sexy.

"Yeah, good to see you too, " I replied.

"Have you been waiting long?"

"Not really. Just a few minutes," I lied.

"Come, let's walk," she volunteered.

We walked along the flower lined paths through the meandering gravel road. Our conversation was limited but lively. We talked about school, the seniors and plans. At one point, I became flustered when she asked about why it had taken so long for us to get together and hang out. I had no rejoinder and no rationale except for my shyness and reticence. She stopped, held my hand and said, "You're silly. I really like you and always wanted to hang with you." She then took my chin pulled it down to her and passionately kissed me. I was taken aback and jerked. But she calmed me and kissed me again. We stayed that way for a few moments and began to stroll again. Past the large tress, the colorful gardens were barely visible in the diminished light while the fountain flowed from a sculpture of a large pelican into a gray bowl. By then it had turned dark, and the bright full moon shown overhead.

"We better go. I'm getting a bit nervous in the dark. Let's go get something to eat. How about some pizza or a burger?" she said.

"One second. I got something in my shoe" I replied stopping to kneel down to remove the shoe and pebble. I then grabbed her, pulled her down to me, looked carefully about for another human near and kissed her. She responded as I would have suspected. I pulled the Henckles steak knife out of my jeans and slashed her face. She looked at me in shock and terror, her eyes open wide and glaring and her mouth shaped in an "O". I muffled her one scream as I slid the knife across her neck. She gasped and blood started spurting everywhere. As she lay on the ground, I removed her blouse and bra and stared at her young barely formed breasts. I had an orgasm without touching myself from the sheer excitement of what I was doing. I then carved a cross on her breastbone with extreme care and detail. It was done. I had done it. I stood up, looked at her and started to cry. What have I done? But there was no remorse, no turning back. My mission was fulfilled. My desire had been met. I walked away, relieved but conflicted, satisfied but distressed, content but needing more.

Chapter 2

I arrived in New York on July 25th in an intense heat wave. I registered at the Columbia freshman dormitory having been given special permission to move in early. The room was the typical dorm room enclosed by drab appearing walls, furnished with a bed, dresser, and desk with an LED lamp enclosed. My posters and paintings ought to help enliven this place, I thought. Having unpacked and filled the dresser with my clothes, I exited the room ran down the steps and walked outside into the smog, humidity and heat. I wanted to get my bearings and to locate the direction to my new office and internship at "New", which was located on Sixty-Sixth and Broadway, only forty-eight blocks from the Columbia dormitory Realizing that the two- and half-mile walk would be prohibitive in this heat, so I took the bus. Disembarking the bus at Sixty- Eight Street, I waited for the traffic light to change when a young woman brushed by me.

"Excuse me," she said.

"Quite ok."

"You look nice enough. My name is Jennifer," she followed.

"Nice to meet you, too. I'm Evan," I replied.

She was a pretty, petite, dark skinned and haired twenty- something girl, Dressed appropriately for the weather in a tank top and short skirt with leather sandals on her smallish feet.

"Sorry. I can't hang. I'm late for work."

"Where do you work?" Jennifer asked.

"I'm doing an internship at "New" magazine starting today," I acknowledged.

"Wow. That is so cool. I love that magazine."

"Thanks," I replied. "See ya."

I walked the two blocks to the building looking back to see Jennifer looking back at me with a "so long" wave. The building on Sixty-Eighth Street was a modern glass and steel edifice with an expansive marble lobby. I walked into the elevator and pressed twenty-four. The door opened to the "New" suites. Introducing myself to the receptionist, I asked for Anthony Fable, the copy editor. She directed me to Room 2404A, the copy-editing desk. I knocked on the door and walked in after Anthony's acknowledgement from behind the door.

"Hi. I'm Evan Dicks from Beaumont, Mass."

"I'm pleased to meet you. Come on over and let's schmooze," he said in typical New Yorkese The copy editor was a heavy-set man of fortyish with a barrel chest and receding hairline of brownish hair. He wore wire rimmed glasses on his wide nose tipping downward. His hazel eyes were slanted downward and droopy. He was dressed in typical Silicon Valley type garb wearing jeans, a T and a blue work shirt.

"Hi. My name is Anthony Fable. As you can probably appreciate, I'm the copy editor at "New" I've been here for five years so am well versed in the magazine and the company. I'm glad you're helping out this summer. Your resume was outstanding, and we've been looking forward to you joining us."

"Thank you so much. I am pleased to be here and thanks you for the opportunity."

We further discussed my role and schedule. I was to be an assistant copy editor, reviewing technological and scientific articles and slowly getting involved in the creative arm of the magazine. As I suspected this would be a perfect marriage of my two major interests: Science and Journalism. I was to review the articles for content, accuracy of the science and technology and veracity of the references. I spent the rest of the morning getting acquainted with the staff and the workplace. I tried to act as gregarious and outgoing as possible but did appreciate some hesitation in some of the staff, nonetheless. At 1pm, I walked outside to get lunch. Waiting for the light to change on sixty-sixth, I felt a tap on my shoulder. There she was again.

"Hey. Nice seeing you again, eh?"

"Yeah, nice seeing you, too. Are you always just hanging around this corner?" I asked.

"Ah, yes, Evan. No! Coincidence I guess," Jennifer replied. "Would you like to sit down and get some coffee or something to eat?" she continued.

"Cool!" I said.

We crossed the street to a small café and ordered. I chose a salad and tea while Jennifer ordered a hamburger and a diet coke. Our conversation centered around how we came to be in NY this summer and our plans. Jennifer was from a small town in Iowa. Her parents were farmers, but she never intended to stay in Iowa or be a farmer. She never intended to marry a local boy. Her ambition was the theater and films. After graduating from the University of Iowa, she moved to New York to pursue that dream and was having a hard time finding work. Her auditions were well received but she had yet to win a job. She never did reveal the rest of her true life. I later learned her real name was Katie Burch. She was twenty-three years old. She arrived in New York knowing no one and with little financial support. Having a pretty voice and competent ability on the guitar, she was able to earn a small living, singing in local coffee houses and restaurants and had rented a small apartment in the Village until the owner of the Backstreet Java House, one of her often-frequented venues, offered her a permanent gig and a place to crash. Having little resources and no other New York acquaintances, she accepted with reservation. Her initial instinct was correct as within three months she was addicted to cocaine and walking the streets as his "girl."

Not knowing her life story, sitting at the table opposite her, I kept wondering what this pretty girl was doing here with me? What was her real story? We continued our conversation. I spoke about my own life, my town, my friends, high school graduation and my New York job. We chatted for another thirty minutes when I excused myself stating that I had to return to work. She looked at me with understanding sad eyes and suggested we meet again that night or at some future time. I looked back at her, "Are you serious? You really want to hang with me?"

"Sure. You seem nice and I need a friend in New York," she answered.

We agreed to get together the following night at the coffee house where she performed.

"That way we can hang out and you can see me play. I'll play a song just for you. It'll be great fun!" she exclaimed.

Work the following day was difficult to navigate in anticipation of my "date" with "Jennifer." I reviewed an article on a new App for a smartphone. It was a mathematics application to help calculate the caloric needs of individuals at various times of the year and during various activities. The obvious role would be in weight control. The article was well written and accurate, but I wasn't sure the App would be very popular or successful. I told the copy editor, Anthony of my reservations but he cautioned me about the role of the copy editor. It was to edit the piece and not to judge its relevance or salability. The article had already been accepted by the editorial staff. The rest of the day passed very slowly but without difficulties.

At 6pm, I left the office building and took the subway to W. 8th street to Backstreet Java House. I sat at a small table ordered a French roast coffee with a ham sandwich and waited for Jennifer's set to begin one and a half hours later. Lingering over the coffee with a new novel I had just begun "Deadly Motivations" a medical thriller about a viral epidemic, the time passed rapidly. At 8pm, the MC announced the folk star Jennifer, using only the name I knew her by.

Jennifer sang a number of covers including "Both Sides Now"' and "Diamonds and Rust" and two originals entitled, "Here I Am" and "Uptown." After receiving modest applause for the barely twenty people there, she strolled to my table and sat down on one of the metal chairs.

"Hey. Thanks for coming," she said.

"I told you I would. Didn't you believe me?"

"Ah, yes I did, it's just nice to see you," she replied.

We sat and chatted until her second set, which was very similar to her first but performed in front of fifty people this time. Stepping off the stage to perfunctory applause, she waved to me while she disappeared backstage, and I followed to wish her farewell.

"Great show, Jennifer," I acknowledged.

"Thanks again for coming," she called out to me from a group of well-wishers. "Don't leave yet. I want to speak to you."

"OK," I said and waited in the crowded smoky basement.

After thanking and greeting the few around her, she walked over to me, kissed me on the cheek and suggested we leave.

"Where are we going?" I asked.

"To my apartment," she answered.

"Huh?" I questioned with astonishment.

"You'll see."

We walked the six blocks to her West Village apartment and climbed the three flights to enter an old two room flat. The kitchen and eating parlor were confined to one room and the bedroom was through a door a few feet away. There was an old stove with an oven below it, a small refrigerator with a white enamel facade and a round wooden table with four bentwood chairs around it. The main room served as the dining room and the kitchen. I didn't enter nor was I shown the bedroom but suspected it had the same antique feel to it.

Sitting down while she boiled water for coffee, I said facetiously, "This is a nice place."

"Are you shitting me? This is a dump, but beggars can't be choosers. My friend, the manager of the club, lets me crash without rent."

"I don't understand all this. You're here in New York without any friends or prospects, living in this fucking dump. Why?"

"I'm going to be an actress. It takes time. I have to endure the bad before the good. Don't you understand that?"

"But you're young with a college degree. Why don't you find something more substantial than singing in that small coffee house for pittance and living here with that manager dude?"

"It is the way it is," she replied without further explanation.

She then invited me into the bedroom. I was taken aback and declined staring at her astonished look of disbelief.

"You're sure? We can have a nice time."

"No thanks," I repeated the refusal.

She accepted the fact and became reticent afterwards. Our conversation was limited and, we exchanged very few thoughts afterwards as I arose to leave. She rushed over and gave me a hug which surprised me. I looked at her stunned, "What is it?"

"I wish I could talk to you more about what's inside of me, what I'm feeling and going through, but you're so young and naïve. Thanks anyway. I'll see you."

"Yeah, see ya," I repeated opening the door and exiting the dilapidated apartment to a rickety old stairwell with stained granite stairs. Halfway down the stairwell, I abruptly pivoted and returned the half flight to her door. I knocked twice before she responded. As she opened the door, I realized what I feared, the force, the urge was driving me and propelling me against my will. My mind shouted... "No, No." But I moved on. I saw her in her flimsy nightie and kept moving forward. She grabbed at my neck and face. But I moved on. I found the kitchen knife and didn't hesitate further in spite of her protestations and her resistance. I looked into her terrified eyes but didn't waver. I grabbed the knife and moved it slowly across her throat. Blood spurted as she screamed while she slowly turned pale and weakened, I felt the release. I felt that beautiful calming, endorphin loaded release. That pleasurable feeling which nothing could duplicate was beyond description. I completed the task and then marked her chest with the long cross. I watched as she whimpered and succumbed. Then came the usual sad, guilty remorse.

I ran out the door, checked the stairway for intruders and ran down those rickety stairs and out the door to the dark humid night. I had to somehow change my clothes and avoid any contacts. But I was more than four miles from my dorm room. Before I hailed a cab, I hid my blood-stained clothes as best I could in multiple nearby receptacles. When we reached the Columbia dormitories, I ran out of the cab and up the stirs of the dormitory. I finally reached my room and collapsed on the bed, exhausted, confused and frightened. My mood was as dark as the room; I stared at the ceiling and noticed the reflections of the streetlamps below. As my mind raced, I recounted the past few weeks and what I had done. I questioned my actions and the motives that led to them. But I was acting without control. Something was driving me and pulling me in this direction. Again, fear crept into my psyche and melancholy pervaded my mood. I closed my eyes, tried to sleep but the horrors of Jennifer's death and the terror etched in her face prevented any hope of sleep. I continued awake, alone until the sun of a new day arose.

I remembered the previous night. Horrified I thought about the knife. What had I done with it? Searching the room, I found the blood-stained chef's knife lying on the floor. I scrubbed it clean and took it with me when I left for my job. I would have to find a good place to hide it or better yet destroy it.

Chapter 3

Capt. Captree was summoned to Beaumont arboretum by one of his police officers when the body of Emily O'Connor was discovered the morning after her death. He had spent the last few weeks investigating the circumstances of the murder without an apparent perpetrator. The name of Evan Dicks did come up. He learned that Emily and Evan had danced at the party and had been talking that evening. But everyone dismissed Evan as a possible suspect. His introversion, demure personality, aloofness and eccentricity marked him an unlikely murderer. This was obviously a pre-meditated act with a possible "religious" motive. Captree's interrogation methods led to shock, and indignation at this heinous crime. Emily was a poster child for the perfect, well adjusted, mature teenager-pretty, well liked and well adapted and very popular. Why would anyone want to kill her and then deface her body in such a monstrous, repulsive fashion? Was there a secret part of her personality that she kept hidden and that only a few knew about? Captree's investigation led to no such conclusion, but yet he was unconvinced and irresolute. His conversation with Emily's parents was especially difficult and distressing. They were inconsolable and certainly, at the thought that Emily might somehow be at fault.

"What the fuck are you talking about? You can't stand here and give me this shit. I don't give a crap what you think. To instigate such an atrocious act is unconscionable. I don't care what the circumstances are or the personality of the victim," shouted Emily's father, William at Captree.

"I agree. But we still have to find a motive and have to investigate all possibilities. If there was a dark side to Emily, at least we can begin to search out those associated," replied Captree.

"Get the fuck out of my house" William O'Connor said dismissing the sergeant.

"I'm so sorry," remarked Captree leaving the O'Connor's and realizing the error of his line of investigation at this time and with the parents of the victim. Nor was this the day to pursue this conversation any further.

I was now well into my internship and seemingly doing very well garnering positive reports from my superiors. I completed the summer internship in an archetypal fashion. Many co-workers did remark that I should let loose and be more genial and energetic, less insular and reserved, that being the only way to truly enjoy New York. I acknowledged their remarks, but I remained the proverbial loner, keeping to myself and not volunteering much about my life. I built a wall and did not allow anyone to enter. When finally it was time to enter college and bid adieu to the staff at "New", I continued in the same manner with undo fanfare.

"It was a pleasure having you with us this summer," remarked Anthony Fable as I proceeded around the office to say my perfunctory farewells.

"Yes. Thank you for being so helpful and kind. I hope I didn't interfere with your work," I answered.

"Don't be absurd. You were great," responded Fable.

I rushed out of the office and headed back to the dorm to prepare for orientation. Waiting at the light to cross Broadway, I felt a sudden tap on my shoulder.

"Hey. Where you going? Wait one minute. I need to talk to you", the stranger said as he turned me around forcefully.

"I, I, I was crossing the street."

"Well. We need to talk," the stranger said.

"I can't. I'm late for school."

"Bullshit. Follow me or you're in deep shit."

I followed him haltingly and then ran across the street dodging the traffic and running toward Columbia's campus. I had no idea who this stranger was, but I wasn't waiting around to find out.

Chapter 4

Registration and orientation at Columbia were dramatic. I thoroughly enjoyed the "Ivy League" manner. Of course, I was invited to all the social events. The president's greeting party was at his magnificent Upper West Side penthouse. This was reserved for the Scholar group, that prestigious, high achieving student contingent that was admitted to the special program with specific academic goals in mind for the future. At the gathering, I met many of my contemporaries and was duly impressed with their accomplishments. I didn't fraternize much but was brought into multiple conversations- politics, sociology, science, psychology and economics being discussed by America's future leaders. I felt misplaced but having been invited, I guessed I belonged. The head of the English department approached me having met me during my visit to the campus last autumn. And remembering the essay I wrote about my intentions to study American literature.

"Hey, aren't you Evan Dicks. It's so good seeing you here. I wasn't sure you had accepted our offer of a place in the freshman class."

Surprisingly but courteously, I replied, "Yes, I am, Evan. I am so astonished that you remembered me or my name."

"Don't be. I take more than an active interest in the "stars" and those who have great potential. How are you enjoying your first few days here?" the chairman asked.

"Thank you so very much and indeed, this is great, and your photographic memory is astonishing and appreciated," I stated and continued, "This is a beautiful home and what a view!"

"I agree. But not all of us live in this splendor. We plebes live the meager life," laughingly remarked the fiftyish bald headed, overweight stout gentleman standing in front of me.

Anything I can help you with? Or if there is anything you need or have questions about, my office door is always open."

"No. I am fine for now."

"Well then carry on."

As he walked away, I looked for a place to go or hide so I walked to the windowed wall facing the Hudson and admired the view. The Jersey side glistened with lights illuminating the entire skyline. I looked north and surveyed the GW Bridge and then looked south to glimpse the buildings of Hoboken jutting out over the river. As my thoughts rambled back to Jennifer and to then Emily, a thin co-ed no more than five feet tall with a shock of black hair cut short approached me.

"Hi," she said.

"Hey!"

"How are you?"

"My name is Sara, Sara Fried."

"I'm Evan Dicks."

"Pleased to meet you. Isn't this place unbelievable? I just love this apartment. It is so gorgeous, enormous and beautifully appointed and that killer view. Wow!!

"Yeah. The presidency of Columbia University is surely a well-paid gig, eh?" I remarked.

"You'd say so. Where are you from?" she asked trying to make conversation. But I was hardly interested. Trying to cut our conversation short but not being impolite, I replied, "Massachusetts near Boston."

"I'm from right here in the Big Apple."

"That's great. If you'll excuse me, I have to meet someone," trying to be genteel but dismissive at the same time.

"Oh! That's quite all right. Go ahead."

I left and engaged another group in conversation as if I belonged. When it became apparent, she lost interest, and went to another area of the apartment, I stepped back to the area around a grand piano where a group was doing Beatles covers and I joined.

"Ah! Look at all the lonely people," they sang as I thought about myself and my own loneliness and psychological dysfunction.

I moved towards the door. Reaching for the knob, turning to look at the living room and the assembled, I noticed her. She was medium height with brown hair, a sculpted face not overly beautiful but pretty, nonetheless. She was in an animated conversation with a group of others that I paid little attention to. My focus was solely on her: Her intelligent eyes, exaggerated hand movements and conviction of her voice. Why did I dwell on her? What was I thinking? No, I said to myself but hardly convincingly.

After the short walk to the dorm, I reentered my room and flipped on the TV. The NEWS channel ticker read:

Breaking News: Killer remains at large. Detectives continue to search for any clues to the mysterious death of a twenty-three-year woman stabbed to death in the East Village.

The reporter speaking to the detective asked probing questions with little substantive response. "Yes. We continue to gather all the clues and witnesses."

"But this has been ongoing now for quite a few weeks?"

"We have learned some things, but I am not privileged to relate those to the media," the detective responded.

"Can't you tell us anything? There is a growing concern. Have you identified the victim? Is she from New York? Do you believe this is the first of many killings? Is there a serial killer on the loose?"

The detective looked at the reporter with abhorrence and glaringly said, "No further question. I'm sorry. Now if you'll excuse me, I have to go!!"

"There you have it ladies and gentlemen. This case remains wide open with very little forthcoming from the NYPD. There remains an unsolved gruesome stabbing of a young woman whose identity has not been released and a neighborhood under a vail of apprehension and fear and a community in extreme distress!!"

I snapped the TV shut and sat on the bed, holding my throbbing head in my hands, mortified but with gratification and a little remorse or sorrow. I tried closing my eyes and falling asleep knowing full well that it was a useless and futile exercise. What drove this madness? Why did I get that rush from these acts? The question lingered in my mind as I succumbed to sleep.

Chapter 5

I awoke the next morning looking forward to the day's activities. We were to have another orientation meeting. This time it was for the English Department. By the time I arrived, the gathering numbered well over fifty students. It was held at Chandler Hall, with its occupancy of one hundred and twenty-six seats nearly filled. At the lectern was the chairman, Prof. Michael Kates. I looked around the room at the wide eyed, anxious and anticipatory faces. I thought these are some of the brightest kids in the country and here I am sitting alongside them. I scanned the room for a few more moments when I saw her. That same girl I noticed the night before. She was halfway up the room towards the left aisle. I tried to quickly turn away so she wouldn't notice my "eyeing" and staring at her, but I was too late. She acknowledged my gaze with a smile. I smiled and turned to the front of the room and listened to Prof. Kates.

I am excited to welcome you to Columbia University. As you well know you have been selected from a very elite group of high schoolers. I am also thrilled that you have chosen English as your major. Our curriculum is a most rigorous one with a very intense list of prerequisites. But I guarantee you that this list will serve you well in your major and in your life. We have tailored the list to coincide with your chosen fields. You will find it challenging and time consuming but well worth your investment in time and study. After my introduction, I would like you to break out into modules to meet the professors who will discuss their varied curricula. These sections were chosen by what we have gleaned from your personal statements indicating your current intentions. I expect this may very well change in the future, but for now we'll proceed in this manner. I very much want to remind you that we are a most congenial department, and my door is always open for question or any difficulties either personal, academic or with a professor, you may have. The work is difficult and arduous but also can be fun and most definitely enlightening. I wish you again the best of luck and see you on campus.

I was directed to a room in Philosophy Hall with approximately twenty-five other freshmen. To my surprise, she was there. She waved me over. I sat beside her and was tongue-tied, not knowing how to proceed. She commenced the conversation to my relief.

"Hey, weren't you at the president's party last night? I thought I noticed you."

"Yes, I was. I did see you as I was leaving."

"My name is Peg Myrtle."

"I'm Evan Dicks. Are you from New York?"

"Hardly. I'm from McCork, Nebraska. Small town Midwestern hick you might say."

Mc who?"

"Oh!" she said with a laugh. "It's a small farming town in Southwest Nebraska."

"How the hell did you end up in Harlem, New York?"

"I wanted to go to a big city. Get away from the small-town life of the Midwest and see what I was missing my whole life. I'm interested in writing and journalism and thought Columbia offered the best of both worlds, big city life in an amazing university with an excellent journalism school, thus, giving me the best chance to succeed. I guess you're a big city native."

"No. Not really. I come from a suburb of Boston called Beuamont, but I do get into the city quite often."

"What brings you to Columbia?"

"It was the best school I got accepted into. Although truthfully, it was one of my first picks because of the English department and the prestigious journalism school also. I guess my intentions are also to become a writer."

"That makes us two peas in a pod. Sorry, that was infantile and corny and not all in the sophisticated manner of an Ivy Leaguer."

"No worries. I find it kind of cute and innocent. Kates did say that we're split into the breakout sessions according to our academic introductory profile and our future intentions."

"Yes. He did."

At that point the professor called the assembled to order and commenced discussing his curriculum. More importantly, he emphasized what one can expect at Columbia and how difficult the prerequisite course work is. He stated that the reading list is enormous and impossible to complete. But he told us not to fret. No one finishes the required readings totally and still gets by. He emphasized that he himself had only read approximately one half of the total assigned books and most of the freshman in his class didn't even complete that much. The group laughed and someone asked if he used Cliff Notes.

"Don't ever divulge that you do and never use any of the language from those rags. The profs know all the tricks and all the synopses and will heavily penalize you if you are discovered."

"Just joking," replied the questioner.

"Yes. I know but I had to warn you anyway."

He discussed some other erudite topics that bored most of the students and then dismissed us.

"See you in class," he said to no one in particularly.

As I left the classroom, Peg walked over to me. "Cup of coffee?" she asked.

"Sure!" I replied but not really sure if I wanted to engage in further conversation with her.

She was nice enough and pretty and obviously innocent enough. But the state of my psyche confused me. Did I really want to start a relationship? Could I trust my emotions and my mental state? Was she going to be another victim? I was again torn as I was in my previous female encounters.

We walked the four blocks to the Starbuck's on Amsterdam and 118th street. I ordered a tall cappuccino and she a tall latte. The coffee house was filled with students, area residents and some straddles ordering at the counter. You could tell this was a university coffee shop by the din and lively conversations. I particularly noticed two young long haired and bearded individuals playing rapid chess. Must be profs at the school I thought without commenting.

"This is so great," she stated emphatically. "I just love the atmosphere of this college. So urban but yet with a hometown feel."

"Hometown? Is this what McCork feels like? Interesting. I would have guessed that the local food establishments would be much less diverse and less crowded."

"I was only suggesting that there seems to be a unique camaraderie here, similar to what you would expect in a small town. But mostly I'm impressed with the intelligentsia," she answered defensively.

"Yes, I agree typical small towns have comradeship? But nothing else in this coffee shop reminds of small-town life."

"Oh! Indeed. I agree. But this just stimulates me so much more than the typical farm work chatter, the issue of paramount importance in McCork. Here the world is the polemic and not the local fair," she stated cautiously, not knowing what my response might be.

"I understand and I agree, this is a very stimulating environment, and I am very happy to be here."

"Me too. Are you going to the mixer tonight? I was thinking that the days of freedom are down to a precious few and I wanted to have as much fun as possible until classes started.

"Probably," I stated with some hesitancy that she picked up on and replied. "Oh!! You have got to come. Who am I going to know otherwise?

I smiled and nodded.

We continued to nurse our coffees for the next hour then arose and headed back to campus. When we approached her dormitory, she invited me up to see her room and possibly meet her roommate. I looked into her eyes felt that unforgiving sensation, hesitated and declined.

"Ok then, see you tonight," she yelled back to me as I walked back toward my dorm. Looking back, I nodded again.

Chapter 6

It was well past ten, by the time Ronald Captree turned the key to his front door. As he entered Claudia, his thirteen-year-old daughter came in to greet him. She was a tallish, plumpish teenager of well-defined facial features. Some would probably call her pretty, but he looked at her as being attractive not gorgeous or beautiful but the image of her mom. Capt. Captree had been raising her for the past two years alone. Thus, she usually stayed home until he returned from work. Claudia's mom, Veronica had been killed by a rapist in New York two years ago. The rapist/killer was apprehended. Although evidence was not confirmatory, he confessed to the murder following a grueling and contentious interview and is now serving a life sentence at Attica Correctional Facility in Attica, NY, the site of the famous prison uprising and protest of 1971. As is well known the Attica prison has a reputation for harsh treatment of its inmates with an impenetrable façade with two-foot-thick walls that are thirty feet high with twelve guard towers. The conditions, the poor medical care, the bad food and the lack of rehabilitation programs led to a dehumanizing experience for the in mates the resulting in the aforementioned "uprising" and protest.

Ronald Captree couldn't stay in New York any longer after the trial of Dexter Compton, the alleged perpetrator of the heinous murder and rape. The memories of his wife's death and grisly murder and the threats of Compton during the trial were too much to bear and he felt Claudia needed a calmer more serene atmosphere and life. He left his detective job in NY for the bucolic environs of Beumont in a lesser paying job with less responsibility, but a much-improved quality of life. Thinking of this current killing infuriated him thinking stuff like this doesn't happen in Beuamont. He kissed Claudia, who suggested that there was some dinner in the fridge if he wanted. But he felt too fatigued, overwhelmed and frustrated to eat.

"Are you ok?" Claudia asked, noticing his despondent affect.

"Yeah, just a tough day."

"The Emily O'Connor murder, huh?"

"How d'ya guess?" he asked stupidly knowing full well that it was all the town talked about.

Everyone was anxious, apprehensive and fearful, and he felt that burden especially after his encounter with Emily's father. His interrogation and anger were fueled by his own history with a killer and rapist and the elegiac and agonizing investigation at that time. Yes, he agreed, he had been damaged by his circumstance and it has clouded his judgement but there was little alternative to his role in this case as he was the senior law enforcement officer in Beaumont. Unfortunately, he felt remorse and surely didn't want to involve Claudia or take his aggravation out on her, so he quickly went into the den and flipped on the fifty-inch monitor. It flashed the CNN logo with the headline.

Breaking News: Killer remains on the loose.

The story contained details of the NYC Greenwich village murder a woman in her mid-twenties. She was slashed and her throat was slit. He intently watched the rest of the story but saw the similarity to Emily's murder. Maybe a lead! He made sure he noted the location of the precinct and the name of the officer being interviewed although little further information was reported. He would have to contact the NYC Police Department as soon as possible. Impatiently he switched the channel to other news outlets but to no avail as there were no other reports of the NY slaying. He then settled on some puerile reality show which held his interest for the better part of ten minutes. He switched off the TV, picked up the paper and reviewed the mundane items of the Beaumont Gazette, saw nothing of interest and deposited the paper in the recycling bin.

He arose the next morning at 6am prepared a cup of coffee, woke Claudia and sat at the kitchen table, anxious to start his day.

"Morning dad," Claudia strode in cheerfully.

"Morning hon, how did you sleep? What's on the agenda for today?"

"I'm going to hang with some friends after school. Otherwise, not much. Hey dad. Do you mind if I ask you a question? How is the investigation going into Emily's murder? The kids keep asking if there's anything to worry about."

He was startled by her perceptiveness but not wishing to frighten her or create undue stress at the school he replied, "Nah. Indeed, I think this is a singular event. I don't believe there is killer in Beaumont about to commit a string of murders." But not necessarily believing his own words especially after the report her heard last night, he tried to deflect her questions further. "Sorry I have to get going – busy day today. See you tonight."

He drove the four miles to the center of town, passing the tree lined streets the well-manicured lawns and the large imposing homes. What the fuck was he doing in this super wealthy enclave and how could he reconcile his standing in this community. His inferiority complex only heightened his anxiety and lack of progress in uncovering any clues to the killer. But the CNN report gave him some optimism. He felt anxious to get to the office and speak to the NYPD. He waved to some of the bustling town's people as they rushed to start their commute to Boston. He noticed William O'Connor at the train station, waved courteously but received only a curt shrug in return. By the time he entered the Sherriff's office, he could barely contain the enthusiasm of the anticipated contact in NY. He stopped at Doug's Diner for an egg and bacon and cheese sandwich, laughing to himself at the symbolism of this "very NY breakfast" on this hopeful day.

He completed the paperwork and made the phone call that he anticipated all morning.

"Is Detective Francis there, please? This is Capt. Captree in Beumont, Mass."

"Yes. Hold on one minute while I get him," replied Sgt. Mulvaley at the NYPD 6th precinct.

"This is Detective Francis; how can I help you?"

"Good morning, my name is Capt. Ronald Captree. I'm the senior law enforcement officer in Beaumont, Mass. We're a small suburb of Boston if you haven't heard of us. Last night I saw you on CNN describing your investigation into a grisly murder. I wanted to discuss this with you In June of this year, the valedictorian of our high school was killed. Her throat was slashed, and she was molested. It was a gruesome scene. In addition, a cross was carved over her heart. This MO seems to approximate the murder you discussed last night?"

"Holy shit. Yes, it does. Our victim was a young woman in her twenties whose throat was also slashed. She was molested posthumously. She also had a cross carved over her heart at her breast. I agree, it all sounds very suspicious, but I think it is too soon to jump to the conclusion that this is a serial occurrence. We're only talking about two instances two hundred and fifty plus miles apart. How could we possibly connect two murders identically committed at that distance?"

"I think that that would be fairly clear that the killer traveled from Beaumont to NY."

"Yes, that makes sense. But we're talking about a population of what twenty-five to thirty thousand. It would be like finding a needle in a haystack."

"I understand but it is a start. Why don't you investigate your population as to movement in the last three months: including movement out of Beaumont to NY, plane reservation to NY and, of course, Amtrak reservations? I'll check the schedules on this end. Of course, this will be a daunting task but at least we have an initial clue. We had nothing else up until this point. Can you come down to NY to discuss this further?"

"I'm sorry, I have a thirteen-year-old that I can't leave, but maybe we can take a weekend in NY. How does that sound?"

"Great. Will this weekend work?"

"Yes. I'll call later today or tomorrow with further details."

After he hung up, he called Jim Martin, the stout, humorous sergeant, who was his right-hand man detailed the conversation he just had with Detective Francis. He related the gruesome murder of the NY woman and especially the slashing of the throat and the cross over the heart.

"Wow. Some coincidence."

"Coincidence??" Captree remarked astonishingly.

"Well. I guess maybe more of a pattern, huh?" sheepishly responded Martin.

"Yea, I guess!! I want you to check the airlines for Beaumont folks that flew to NY in the last three months. Also, we'll need to check the Amtrak schedules for NY from Beaumont or connecting from Beaumont to Boston to NY. There's got to be a clue there or at least a connection. Meanwhile, I'm going to drive down to NY to meet Francis. It would be nice to get a profile of the victims to search for a connection. Maybe if lucky there is DNA that we could match.

The trip to NY with Claudia was pleasant. They left early on a Friday morning on a pleasant, warm August day. Traffic was light and Claudia incessantly didn't stop chattering. She hardly remembered NY but was very glad to accompany her father on this adventure. They drove west on I-84 connecting to I-90 south to I -95 south. They did stop at the Wilmington rest stop on I-90 for a late breakfast and a break.

"Dad, this is great. I love it. I'm having so much fun. I never get to spend this much time with you.

What are we going to do in NY?" Her continuous chatter did not cease. But Captree was delighted with her exuberance although this was tempered by the reason for the trip, which was hardly for entertainment or amusement. They reached NY close to 2pm and drove down the West Side Highway into the Village. He booked a room at the Walker Hotel on W.13th street. The hotel was considered one of the boutique hotels in the Village. It had an art deco décor with two-hundred-square-foot rooms that easily accommodated the twin beds he booked. Its location was central, which he needed for convenience. It was clean, functional and reasonably priced. He would see Det. Francis as soon as they got settled.

Before he left, he mentioned to Claudia to stay in the room until he returned. He warned her of the big city and the dangers it imposes on innocent "small town girls". She acknowledged his warning as he left the hotel for the three-block walk to the 6th precinct on W. 10th Street.

"Detective Francis, please? Capt. Captree to see him."

"Is he expecting you?"

"Yes, he is."

"One moment," responded the sergeant at the reception desk.

Captree was ushered into a back room and at the desk sat a well-dressed mid-sixties bald man and an attractive late thirty something blonde woman.

The middle-aged man spoke first and introduced himself as Det. Francis. The woman followed:

"Hello! I'm Detective Alexandra Saunders." offering her hand.

He shook her hand, "I'm Ronald Captree". I'm here about the murder in Greenwich Village recently. Did Francis clue you in?"

"Yes," she responded seemingly taking the lead and showing superiority over Francis.

"I thought we should discuss this further. As you well know we had a very similar killing in Beaumont in late June with a very similar MO."

"Tell me a little more about your case," she said quizzically.

"The victim was an eighteen-year-old honor student from a prominent Beaumont family. Her father is a renowned Boston surgeon, and her mother is somewhat of bon vivant and a socialite. You know the type, bridge, country club lunches, DAR and *social register*. The daughter was murdered in an isolated park. Her throat was slashed with a large blade. She died almost instantaneously. She was then molested, and a cross was carved over her heart. It was a gruesome, grisly crime, quite unusual for a town like Beaumont. There was blood everywhere. The killer was very professional. Not a trace of evidence was found. There was no murder weapon discovered. There weren't any footprints, fingerprints or significant clues. That is until I heard the story of this seemingly second murder in the Village."

"Interesting that you call it the Village," remarked Alexandra Saunders.

"Well! Um. Yes. I was once a NY detective.

"Captree? Captree?" bemused Francis. "Oh! Wait! I remember. You worked the 17th. Wasn't your wife murdered two or so years ago."

"Wow, what a memory."

"Well, it was a famous case that made headlines in all the local *rags*."

"I guess," said Captree. "Anyway, from what I understand your case is similar, no?"

Saunders spoke up," Very. Same MO except our victim is a vagabond. She lives in this decrepit apartment owned by a local coffee house owner. We think she supports herself with prostitution, but she had never been arrested so we're not sure. Her landlord doesn't know what she did, but he let her stay in the apartment for nominal rent in exchange for performing at his club and doing odds and ends. For all we know, he was her pimp, but we have nothing on him or a criminal record to support that impression. She came to NY from the West like Utah in search of a musical and acting career according to her parents but like with all young naïve women, the city swallowed her up and spit her out."

"I guess you didn't find any evidence of DNA or fingerprints or a weapon either, but I find it strange," said Captree.

"What do you find so strange?" asked Francis.

"The victims are so unlike each other. I would think if we're dealing with a serial killer, the victims would be very similar. A certain type that the killer finds the need to eliminate or punish."

"I'm not sure about that. Whatever is driving his killing, the so-called trigger may have been exhibited by both women even though they are unlike each other. For instance, the prompt could be imagined or definitive sexual perversion," stated Saunders.

Now Captree understood why she was there at this meeting. She was the head of the Sexual Assault Unit at the Downtown NYPD precincts and was well versed in its technicalities having a BA from NYU in sociology and studying for a Masters in Sexual Criminology.

"You have to remember that women can very well initiate an aggressive act without realizing as much. To an individual with a fragile psyche harboring resentment toward women even a friendly gesture can elicit such a maniacal response. Serial killers and rapists very commonly have a deep seeded hatred for women, negative feelings, harbored for many years, against their mothers even to the degree of hatred. Sometimes it is related to a sense of lack of love or by a competition with their fathers, who inevitably win that struggle. I'm sorry. Am I getting too Freudian? I was just making the point it is not what a woman looks like or what she does but rather how she acts."

Her knowledge and the dissertation impressed Captree so to be at a loss for words.

"I understand and wholeheartedly take your lead on this as you seem so knowledgeable, he suggested."

"I've been studying and working in this field for quite a long time," remarked Saunders.

"Ha! At your age you couldn't have been doing much of anything for quite a long time!"

"I'm older than I look."

With this remark Captree seemed to detect a chemistry between them. but he hardly could act on it even if it was there. He looked at her and smiled and received a knowing nod in return.

"Ok. What else have we got here to go on?" asked Francis.

"I have my deputy checking airline and busses and Amtrak for travel between Beaumont, Boston and NY. We'll see if that turns up any clues."

"Good," said the beautiful blonde encyclopedia. "We'll have to meet again."

"I have to get back to Massachusetts tomorrow, but I'll surely be in touch if anything turns up and I would hope you would do the same."

"Indeed. Thank you," they said in unison.

He left the precinct and returned to the Walker knocked on the door of Room 605 but there was no response. He knocked again, nothing and said, "Shit." He slid the keypad into the slot, opened the door and stared at an empty hotel room.

Dexter Compton opened the note he received on the daily mail rounds. He looked for a return address but there was none. He knew who sent it by what it read: "Done."

Chapter 7

As the sun slowly washed into evening, I started realizing that Peg Myrtle was a good sort but was I going to get involved? I doubted my true intentions, my motivations or my fragile psyche. Could I carry on a normal relationship? Or would the demons raise their ugly specter and reduce me to the psychopath I knew I was? I put on a blue oxford and tight jeans with a wide belt and black sneakers, looked in the mirror and saw the reflection of a taut face with limited expression, side- parted hair and brown eyes that seemed to lack sparkle. I realized that the nerd I was just a few months ago seemed to be changing into a more confident individual. I headed out to the Francis S. Levien Gymnasium where the mixer was being held thinking, *Am I really doing the right thing? Is this what I really want? Is this girl right for me or even good for me? Or am I only pursuing my demons?* Recognizing someone from orientation snapped me out of those thoughts, I tapped him on the shoulder.

"Sorry," I said to no response, but he moved on as if I wasn't there or had not knocked him." "The Invisible Man," I thought, which at times I felt.

I walked into Columbia's huge fieldhouse which serves as the men's and women's basketball and volleyball home field. A DJ was playing emo and techno rock which I really didn't enjoy. I looked around the room not wanting to find anyone I knew as I preferred my loneliness. But there she was, and she noticed me before I could duck out.

"Hey, Evan. I'm here!"

"Hey Peg, how goes?" I said non-enthusiastically.

"I am so glad you're here. You can see it would be impossible to know anyone in this mad house or even meet someone. Why don't we sit in the stands and try to talk or even dance if you'd like?"

"I'm not much of a dancer," I answered sheepishly.

"Neither am I, what the fuck it's only for fun not to impress."

Shocked by her flippant use of 'fuck,' I said, "Sure."

The DJ started playing some hip-hop and Peg and I found our way to the center of the gym holding hands. We moved to the beat in some coordinated organized manner which surprised me. This Mid-Western hick was more sophisticated than

I thought, which pleased me, and I followed her lead. We were having a fairly good time dancing to Beyonce, Katy Perry and Taylor Swift, when a ballad, "Hello Stranger" by Yvonne Elliman started. She got up close to me pressed to my chest and started to grind her hips suggestively and with purpose. I was embarrassed by the erection I got and moved back a step, but she inched closer again. As the song ended, she held onto my hand. "That was nice," she said.

I confirmed, "Yes it was. I hope I didn't embarrass you."

"On the contrary. I enjoyed your emotion. I felt turned on also."

I could feel my shame, shyness and unsophisticated immaturity rise, I thought, where *is that confidence?* She seemed so calming, earnest and confident, which helped counter that emotion. We continued to dance and talk between songs and generally become more comfortable with each other. I was surprised by my reaction as this was one of the very few times that I could remember being comfortable with a girl. I became more aware of her inviting mood and attitude as the night progressed. I could feel that she may very well want more of me than I was ready for.

She suggested that we leave and spend some time alone in her room. I hesitated but again was calmed by her reassuring and soothing manner. I acquiesced and we strode out hand in hand. When we entered her dormitory, I suggested that it'd best if I left, but again she demurred as she opened the door and pulled me in. This time there was little doubt about her intentions. She kissed me, moved her tongue around the inside of my mouth and softly moaned. I kissed her, feeling relaxed enough to proceed. She unbuttoned my shirt and took off her blouse exposing well-formed although still young breasts. She slid her hand to my fly and started unzipping my jeans. I gasped and kissed her again full on the mouth with my tongue protruding and meeting hers. I undid her jeans and we fell to the floor. I slowly removed her panties as I stepped out of my jeans.

"Are you sure about this?" I naively asked and remembering our orientation program on proper consent.

"Oh yes, yes. Please touch my pussy. Yes, yes like that!"

We slowly slumped to the floor as my passion and those inner feelings simultaneously returned…

Captree was beside himself. He screamed in the room for Claudia realizing she was not there. He rushed down to the lobby and to the front desk.

"Have you seen by daughter? Claudia Captree? She's not in her room and I emphatically told her to stay put."

"She's the one you came with, about twelve or thirteen. Well, I have to tell you mister you hardly can expect a teenager to stay put when you tell them. No, I haven't seen her since you arrived." said the smarmy desk clerk.

He searched in the lobby, the sundry shop and the café but saw no trace of her. He ran outside gazing in both direction and then ran over to Washington Square Park and again searched up and down the paths with his feared, panicked and dreaded negative result.

He did the only thing he could think of and ran back to the 6th precinct and asked for Detectives Francis and Saunders. When they met Captree burst out, "I don't know where my daughter is. She's missing."

"We're only talking a short time. How do you know she's missing?" commented Francis.

"Claudia is a very responsible youngster, and she wouldn't have left the hotel room without telling me or leaving a note. She's gone and I'm scared shitless. NY is so big and unwelcoming." "Get a grip. You have no idea what happened or even if she's missing. Let's take this one step at a time and not jump to ominous conclusions, OK?" said Saunders with reassuring composure.

"I guess, but I am really frightened, and we were supposed to go back to Beaumont tomorrow."

"Let's do this. We'll start checking around and you go back to the hotel and wait," calmly suggested Saunders.

He finally relented realizing that was exactly what he would have done in the same situation. He headed back to the Walker, went up to his room after again inquiring of the desk whether there was any word from his daughter. After opening the door and flopping down on the bed he picked up the phone and called Jim Martin, his deputy in the Beaumont sheriff's office.

"Hey, Jim" I may be stuck in NY longer than expected. Claudia is gone."

"Gone? What the fuck are you talking about?"

"Yeah! When I got back to the hotel after meeting and speaking to Francis and some detective named Saunders, she was gone. No sign of her. I'm totally panicked and have no idea what the fuck I should do."

"Holy shit. Yeah, yeah you take as much time as you need. Don't worry about us. Everything is under control here."

"Ok, thanks."

"Oh! I almost forgot someone called for you."

"Who? What did they want?" asked Captree.

"He didn't say but did leave a forwarding number."

"What is it? What's the number?" queried Captree anxiously.

Captree wrote the number down and then said, "Thanks. Take care and speak to you soon."

"Yeah! Good luck and make sure you call if you need anything."

After hanging up, Captree dialed the number he had written immediately.

"Yes?"

"Hi, my name is Capt. Ronald Captree. Did you call my office earlier today?"

"Yes! I did," came the voice at the other end.

"Who is this and what do you want? I'm very busy and don't have a lot of time to waste."

"Hmm. I was wandering if you've seen your daughter recently?"

"What? What do you know about my daughter? Who did you say this was?" asked Captree in rapid succession.

"Whoa. One question at a time. Your daughter is safe and with me. I don't intend to harm her but you're going to have to cooperate."

"What? Who is this? Cooperate? Cooperate how?"

Captree heard the click of phone and then the dial tone.

Chapter 8

Falling, falling, twisting, dropping and penetrating the depths, I awoke panting in a cold sweat, gasping as I thought about the recurrent dream of my physical or possible mental demise. Was this repetitive dream of decline a symbol of my mental state or was I dreaming of a possible physical deterioration. I couldn't really differentiate but it mattered little as it was incapacitating. I couldn't sleep and didn't understand what it was that was so frightening to me. Then I remembered the night before. I vividly remembered the passion, the touching and then the penetration followed by that feeling of need and compulsion that I could not control or understand. I remembered grabbing the switch blade, looking into her face seeing the excitement and sexual ardor. Then

I saw the terror as I slashed her throat. Blood started spurting at me, on the bed on the floor and onto the ceiling. I held my hand over her mouth to muffle her screams and watched her eyes open widely with fear and horror at what was happening. Seeing this panic brought on my "release". I watched with little remorse as the color receded form her face. I then carved the cross over her heart. This act was the mental anguish that I obviously was experiencing at night and brought on my nightmares. I obviously was dealing with my previous acts and the obvious need to repeat them. That need and its culmination was what was bothering me. I bolted upright, sat at the edge of the bed and tried to analyze my feelings panting heavily the entire time. I checked the clock. It was 3:11am. What could I possibly do at this hour? Would it be possible to fall back asleep? I put my head back on the pillow with my eyes open and thought about the last few days. My roommate was not in the room, so I wasn't especially careful about being quiet and yelled, "Shit! I'm a fucking mess and I don't fucking see any salvage."

I flipped on my laptop, checked my emails knowing full well no one was sending me any messages. I read the newest headlines, which I found boring except for an item related to a Capt. Captree and his missing daughter. I recognized the name from Beaumont and thought. Why would he be here in NY? I thought of the possibility it had something to do with Emily O'Connor's murder and the murder he heard about the other night of the whore in the Village. This only raised my anxiety further, which surely didn't help my insomnia. I turned off the laptop and declined again onto the pillow. I stared at the ceiling and watched the minutes slowly move. I didn't realize the length of time I stayed in that position, but by the time I checked the clock again, it was 6am. I jumped out of bed, went to the communal shower and took a long shower soaking and staring at the drab tiled stall. I realized that classes were starting today so I headed back to my room to dress. I picked out a white t-shirt and jeans and headed to the cafeteria hoping it was open. Luckily it was. I ordered toast, eggs and coffee and grabbed the first available chair I saw. I sat there nibbling at my breakfast not noticing my surroundings or the people congregating in the cafeteria. They all seemed very eager and animated although I did detect some fretfulness at the start of classes for this mostly freshman gathering.

A student tapped me on shoulder, "Hey. How you doin'? Mind if I sit here?"

"Well, I did want to be alone, but I guess it's ok," I replied.

"My name is Felix," he happily and exuberantly exclaimed.

"Hi. I'm Evan," I responded stoically.

"Math," the bespectacled, short thin teenager said.

I really didn't want to be bothered or carry-on further conversation but needing to be civil., I said,"

I'm an English major." After all this was my first week at Columbia and it didn't make much sense to be anti-social and not courteous.

"That is so cool. You're probably going to have an easy time with the Core, eh?"

"I'm not sure about that. The reading list is pretty daunting."

"Yeh. I guess."

He ate his cereal as we continued to chat, when another student interrupted our conversation.

"Felix." I heard from behind me. It was a pretty co-ed with brown hair, large brown eyes and dark skin and a pretty smile.

"Maria. Hey. Come sit down here."

"Sure," she stated and sat directly in front of me.

"Hi. Who are you?" she inquired politely.

"Oh, shit I'm so sorry this is Evan," blurted out Felix.

"Dicks," I interjected. "Evan Dicks."

"Hiya. I'm Maria Lopez."

"Yeah. Evan is an English major. Maria here is a music major with an English minor but wants to be a journalist," remarked Felix.

"I guess thinking of music criticism, right Maria?" I suggested.

"Yeah. I guess. So, you and I are into the English language, right Evan? That is unusual for me as I was born in Ecuador and English is my second language."

"On the contrary, you're English is superb with no perceptible accent at all. Interestingly I was thinking of writing also," I commented.

"Oh. Thanks. You should hear my parents, though," she answered with a noticeable smile and nod and a discernible twinkle in her eye.

Felix noticed this also and suggested that we all get together again at lunch. I thought about this for a few moments and accepted the invitation. I was thinking of my distraught night and insomnia and thought some friends and company would help and surely wouldn't hurt. I excused myself to head to class across campus.

"Great, we'll be at the taqueria across the street around one or so," said Felix as I arose.

Maria stood also and gave me hug. Detecting some meaning in the gesture, I hugged her back and left noting the time of our lunch.

Peg Myrtle's roommate returned that morning to an awful smell in the hallway. When she unlocked the door, the reason became obvious. Lying on the bed was a nearly decapitated Peg, blood stains throughout, A horrific Peg with a across carved over her heart. Seeing this she let out the most guttural horrific scream that brought some of her floor mates running.

"My God!! Someone help me."

Her neighbor ran over and hugged her trying to calm her down.

"My God, My God, Oh no, Oh no. No, no, no, she again screamed.

She sat on her bed shaking and repeatedly said, Peg, Peg what…?

The resident hall supervisor, a senior ran up to the room and sat with Ellen, the roommate, and waited for the police to arrive. She spoke in a calm, composed and serene reassuring voice, "Be calm. The police are on their way. When did you get in?"

"About 6am or so."

"Did you see anything or anyone or hear anything?"

"No. No. No, I have to get out of here. Please let me go."

"No, you can't. The police are going to want to speak to you. You have to stay," said the supervising senior emphatically.

Over the next five to ten minutes, they spoke sparingly as they waited. Detectives Saunders and Francis arrived as rapidly as they could even though this was the purview of a different precinct. They were called to this scene as it was noted that the murder was similar to a previous one in their precinct in the Village. The crime scene presented a horrifying one. The bloody body sprawled on the bed, naked with a slit throat, there was blood everywhere, the sheets, pillow, ceiling, floor and wall behind the bed. The criminologists were already at work dusting for fingerprints, taking photographs, sampling the area for possible DNA and inspecting the body. Saunders and Francis didn't say much to the assembled, but carefully inspected the body.

Detective Saunders spoke first and asked, "Carl. Do you think maybe we ought to call Captree and let him know since this looks very much like that Beaumont killing and the one in Greenwich Village?"

"I don't know. He's not NYPD but does have some experience. I'm sure he's still in town but in a panic with this thing with his daughter. But, yeah, I guess it would be okay to try."

They asked Ellen, the roommate, to be available in case they needed to speak to her further. They left and headed back to the 6th Precinct. On the way downtown, Alexandra Saunders dialed Captree.

"Ronald Captree here. Can I help you?"

"Captree! This is Detective Saunders. We just got another one."

"Another one?"

"Yeah, another brutal killing. This time it's in a Columba University dorm room."

"Oh, Shit. That could be distressing. It could cause a panic at the school, the dorms and the administration, not to mention the city if publicized.

"I think so. Meet us at the precinct. We should be there in about half an hour."

With my morning classes completed I headed for the taqueria we agreed upon on Columbus Ave. I noticed Maria when I entered but no Felix.

"Hi."

"Hey."

"Where's Felix?" I asked.

"He couldn't make it. There was a murder in his dorm last night and they're questioning everyone on the floor," she replied.

"A murder?"

"Yeah. Some poor girl got her throat slit in her dorm room last night. They say it was absolutely horrible and gruesome. Felix told me that there was blood everywhere. She was naked. Maybe raped and molested. He said it was just a horrific scene."

"Shit. That's shocking. Did you know her?" I said feeling the color drain from my face and my legs becoming wobbly.

"No" she said. "Are you okay? You suddenly don't look so good."

"I-I I think I'm fine just so shocked. Did Felix know her??"

"No. But he did say that he had seen her a few times on the floor in the last few days."

"I guess there are no suspects, yet. Wow, this is really frightful. Is the dorm panicked?" I asked trying desperately to be convincing but not sure whether I was successful.

"I don't know but I'm sure word will spread very rapidly, and the campus will be unnerved and in disarray soon enough."

Captree walked from the Walker to the 6th precinct and beat the other two by almost fifteen minutes. He sat in Detective Francis' office while awaiting their return. He held his head and thought of all the possibilities. Who was it that made that phone call and threatened him and his daughter? He thought of all the offenders that he helped to convict. Only one case was of nebulous reliability.

It had to be Dexter Compton. He would have to contact him although he abhorred doing so. He thought probably the kidnappers would contact him anyway. He was sure Compton wanted retribution or more. But to kidnap his daughter was excessive. He continued this lament when Francis and Saunders walked in.

"Any word on your daughter, yet?" Saunders asked.

"No. But I was just thinking about the identical thing. I might have a clue. There's a guy named "Dexter Comton, who is at Attica. He's the fuck that we convicted of raping and killing my wife two years ago."

"Yes. I remember, but I never heard of the outcome of it. You said that. Compton was convicted. Compton, I know, was a real bad guy. He had a rap sheet a mile long with multiple assault charges and a robbery, but I don't remember any rape or murder charges," interjected Francis.

"Yeah. That's right. We didn't find any physical evidence to link him to the crime, but he eventually confessed under questionable circumstances that his shitty appointed attorney could not overturn or reject. Well anyway I think he might have something to do with my daughter's kidnapping."

"Interesting," commented Saunders. "We'll have to work on this further. Make sure if they contact you again to let us know so we can help you follow-up."

"Anyway. Now let's get to the matter at hand. Shit, that crime scene at Columbia was grisly. This poor young girl's throat was slit, and the same fucking cross was carved on her chest over her heart. She probably was molested also."

"This is so appalling. That's two in NY and one in Massachusetts. Obviously, the killer must still be in NY now. Do you think the perp could be a student at Columbia? That would be something to investigate. There couldn't be too many Beaumont kids that are at Columbia!"

"That's a great idea. Why don't you check that out?" responded Saunders. "But only if you feel up to it given your circumstances."

"No. No. I need to get my mind off this shit with my daughter," Captree said looking despondent and unfocused.

"Not to worry, Captree. Don't bother. We'll handle it," said Francis.

"Yeah. Thanks. But I really don't know what to do with myself. I guess I'll check out Compton. I hate to speak to that son of a bitch, but I don't see a choice. I didn't hear from anyone else since yesterday when they first called."

"You got a phone call from someone regarding your daughter? You should have said something," remarked Francis. "That was really stupid not telling us."

"It was very brief and didn't amount to much. They said that if I want to see my daughter again and unharmed, I would have to follow their direction."

"Shit. That's significant wouldn't you say?" continued Francis.

"I guess," answered Captree acerbically knowing full well that the brief conversation lacked any significant clue as to Claudia's whereabouts or who kidnapped her.

Captree left the office and headed back to the Walker when his cell rang. It was Jim Martin his second in Beaumont.

"They just called again for you and want to speak to you. He said it was urgent!" exclaimed Jim with apprehension and concern.

"Thanks. I still have the number. Same one?

"No. He gave me a different one."

"Ok! By the way, could you please check for any Beaumont students that are registered at Columbia University? There was another killing at a Columbia dorm similar to the Beaumont murder."

"Holy shit. A serial killer on our hands, eh? Sure, I'll get right on it."

Chapter 9

Dexter Compton leaned back on his cot. His ten-by-ten-foot cell seemed especially confining to him today. His big frame barely fit on the small cot. He closed his eyes and thought about his life, which was filled with such early promise. He was a high school football star- the defensive captain of the team with a scholarship to a division I school. Two years of high-profile athletics at Georgia followed that fucking knee injury happened that just wouldn't heal properly. He obviously couldn't cut it in the smarts department. But the real issue was the opioids they gave him for the injury to try to get him back on the field. He thought about his addiction and the money it cost to satisfy it. He remembered all the times that the only way to procure that money was to steal it. But he never killed or raped anyone. That fucking Captree coerced a confession without that damn court appointed attorney objecting or able to overturn it. Somehow the truth had to be realized and Captree was the only one to facilitate. He grabbed the book on his nightstand, opened it to the marked page:

Romans 10:9-10 *"That if you confess with your mouth, "Jesus is Lord," and believe in your heart that God raised him from the dead, you will be saved. For it is with your heart that you believe and are justified, and it is with your mouth that you confess and are saved."*

Yes, he thought, Jesus Christ will save me. "I must believe. I must believe."

His mind raced back to that night- he was strolling down Greenwich, when a siren wailed on the street; two cops rushed out and held him t gun point. They aggressively searched him for what he did not know. His protests were useless as they handcuffed him and pushed him into the RMP (radio motor patrol) and sped to the precinct while reading him his Miranda rights.

"Arrested? What the fuck for?"

"Murder and rape and a detective's wife nonetheless," a sergeant answered.

"Murder? Rape? What the hell are you talking about?"

"We found her on Perry, right around the corner of Greenwich. Someone eyed you."

"Perry?" he asked shockingly. "I haven't been on Perry today at all. I don't understand this shit. Who the fuck eyed me?" he continued in his amazement.

"Just shut up. We'll ask the questions," emphatically stated the sergeant.

That began his nightmarish ordeal that lasted until the trial. The most difficult time was during the interview with Captree. Over and over again screaming at him:

"Tell me what you were doing on Greenwich at 11pm."

"I told you I was walking home from my girlfriend's, who lives in Greenwich."

"So! You were never on Perry, and you have no idea how someone saw you there?"

"No! No!"

But it was useless. After an all-night session without sleep or food, he somehow had said that he might have turned onto Perry. His appointed attorney never questioned the methodology of this "confession," nor did he adequately question Captree. He couldn't afford the bail and thus, remained imprisoned. After three months, that fiasco of a trial followed with his incompetent attorney and that shit Captree testifying about his interview and confession. Yes, he was a convict and had been in prison and did have priors, but goddamn, he was no killer. The investigation was ridiculous. They claimed they couldn't find any DNA and surely didn't find any physical evidence linking him to this crime. But that didn't matter; they had this "eyewitness" that saw a large man on Greenwich, who claimed that the man turned the corner from Perry in a hurry and of course, his "so-called confession" of being on Perry at 11pm around the time of the incident.

Now he is stuck in this shithole Attica, without hope. He does have Jesus and the confidence that somehow the Innocence Project will help him procure DNA to prove his innocence. He thought about asking them to intervene directly but somehow was talked into having Captree speak out on his behalf. He was dismayed that Captree's daughter was kidnapped but that was his brother's idiotic idea. Unfortunately, he was now appended to this miscalculation, which could backfire, but hopefully, Captree will understand, and the Innocence Project will find DNA to test and prove his non culpability.

Captree answered the ringing phone and asked apprehensively, "This is Capt. Captree. How can I help you?"

"In order to get your daughter back you need to ask the lawyers at the Innocence Project to re-open the Compton case. He is innocent and you have to help him. Otherwise, you might never see your daughter again.

"He was convicted in a fair trial, but I can try," Captree responded understanding the request and desperately wanting to get his daughter back.

"Bullshit. Just do it or else," came the ominous return and then silence.

Hearing the silence, Captree disconnected the call and sensing the need for help dialed Saunders and told her what just transpired, "So. I'll guess ask the Innocence Project to intervene and hopefully they deliver on the promise to return her."

"That sounds reasonable. Do you believe Compton killed her?" inquired Saunders.

"I thought so. Yes. But tell you the truth it was all circumstantial. I was a wreck and I needed closure. Thus, I might have taken the interrogation a bit too far in order to get a confession."

"I understand," Saunders said in a calming, reassuring and supportive voice.

Captree then called the Innocence Project and they assured him that they were already aware of the circumstances of this case and would aggressively seek a resolution. He thanked them and hung up. He sat on the bed of the Walker, put his back against the headboard and started to cry. He felt so alone, so distraught and emotional, but at least he felt that his daughter would soon be returned.

As we sauntered down Broadway toward 45th Street, I grabbed Marias's hand. She smiled and held on. We had been friends since that horrific night of Peg's murder. Anthony Fable, my boss and the copy editor at "New" had helped me obtain tickets to "Dear Evan Hansen" at the Music Box Theater. I had wanted to see this beautiful play by Benj Pasek and Justin Paul with a book by Steven Levenson since its opening at the Music Box in 2016. The play, about an alienated neurotic high school student, Evan Hansen, played by Ben Platt, who just happened to also attend Columbia University played Evan, the lead character. The play, the winner of six Tonys including best actor for Ben Platt seemed like a natural for me. A maladjusted high schooler, who creates celebrity for himself by using a tragedy as the impetus, seemed almost biographical. When I mentioned the play to Maria she was as excited as I was. Here we were on our way to see Ben Platt as Evan Hansen and excitedly anticipating the event. I asked her is she'd like a quick dinner since it was still early. She acquiesced and we walked up to 5th Avenue to Little Pizza, which seemed reasonably priced and unpretentious as we would only be sharing a Neapolitan pie and some cokes.

After dinner, we walked down to the Music Box and took our surprisingly fantastic orchestra seats. I mentioned that I would have to send Tony Fable a gift for these wonderful seats. At conclusion of Act 1, I could only imagine the emotional impact the play had on Maria. The suicide of Connor Murphy, a supposed friend of Evan Hansen and the catalyst for the plot of the play by his overdose, in juxtaposition to what was going on at Columbia seemed to cause her to start to cry uncontrollably. We went to the lobby, and I tried to help her compose but found it difficult. She apologized profusely to me, which I reassured her was unnecessary but was nice to hear. We watched the second act pretty much in silence. Leaving the theater, I asked her the obligatory question.

"So, what did you think?"

"Wow. It was fantastic. It completely brought be back to my last year in high school. I knew so many kids just like Evan and Connor. In fact, one of my classmates committed suicide also. That was why I broke down. It just hit home for me and then the killing of Peg really clinched it. Wow, I really loved that play. And what about Ben Platt? Wasn't he utterly fantastic?"

"Yes, indeed, he was."

"Shit. You should have told me. I would have never brought you to this play if that were the case. I didn't want to depress you further than what is already going on at Columbia."

"Oh! No, I really thought it was brilliant and thoroughly enjoyed the evening."

"Yeah. Did you know the Platt went to Columbia?"

"Yes. I did read that. Well. Anyway, Evan, thank you so much for inviting me. It was delightful date: the pizza, the show and of course, you. Thanks again."

"Hey, my pleasure."

We walked down to the subway caught the uptown back to campus and walked towards our dorms. She stopped me when we reached the campus and suggested I come up to her room. I dreaded this. I didn't know how I would react to being with her. I did know I liked her and that she was almost perfect-smart, pretty, garrulous, energetic and engaging, but what about me? What about my psyche. Was I stable enough for a relationship, which had eluded me previously? I hesitated and she was taken aback. "Hey. I like you. It's quite alright to be with me. I want to". She obviously was thinking in terms of consent that we had heard so much about in orientation. Columbia even went as far as to give us a mandate to read Donna Freitas' Consent on Campus- A Manifesto, in which she argues that consent teaching in the university setting is totally inadequate and needs a culture change. Laughing to myself, I thought consent has never been my issue. There was absolutely no doubt about my intentions.

"Not tonight. I'm really tired and would just like to rest," I told her as we walked to her building. "But I'll see you tomorrow."

"OK. That's fine. But I guarantee you, you don't know what you're missing. Have you never heard of Latin lovers?" she laughingly said. I noticed a twinkle in her eye as she kissed my cheek and ran upstairs to her room.

I let her walk up a halfway up the floor and yelled to her, "Hey, can a capricious college freshman change his mind?"

She smiled back, "Absolutely."

Feeling for the knife in my pocket a ran after her two steps at a time.

Chapter 10

I was dreaming of the first time. I distinctly remembered that feeling, that need and the release that I sensed right afterwards. My mind was trying to erase it, but it was too powerful and overwhelming. It completely encompassed my being. It was as if I was another person, another being that needed that sensation. But the hesitancy and ambivalence, I was experiencing, might have been responsible for the long interval between attacks, but deep down I knew I had to experience that sensation again and more than likely again and again:

We were on a college tour of the Northeast at the time. My father wanted us to go to NY alone without mom or James, but I resisted fearing his temper and the possible consequences if I displeased him, especially without Mom as an intermediary. Consequently, the trip started with his annoyance, and things only worsened on the way. His irritation spilled over to a screaming match with my mother and finally silence for about two of the five-hour trip. The time in NY was not much better. We first scheduled Columbia, which my father deemed an "adequate "college for his son, and then NYU, which was hardly acceptable to him so our visit there caused pandemonium. I really enjoyed the visit and thought the school and the metropolitan campus would be ideal. I was almost assured of a scholarship and being enrolled in the prestigious Presidential Honors Scholars Program. In addition, there was the Tisch Drama School, which could very well afford be a venue for possible future playwriting training be it screenplays, teleplays or even serious plays. But Thomas Dicks would not hear any of it. NYU was below him and hence, below his son.

When we returned to the Parker Meridian on W. 56th, he was nearly irreconcilable.

"You are not going to fucking NYU. I don't give a shit about the Scholar program or the fucking theater. My son is going Ivy or nothing."

"But!!"

"Shut up. Not another word, ok?"

My mother hesitatingly said, "Tom, Evan is the one going to college. Not you. Can't you even listen to him? He never said NYU was a fait accompli. He only mentioned it as a choice, an, option. It's an excellent school and it would be a free ride. Why are you so headstrong and uncompromising?"

"Don't give me that crap. The little shit never listens to a word I say."

With that he grabbed my collar pulled me to him, slapped my face twice and shouted emphatically, "Are we clear?"

I looked into his wrathful eyes and convulsed body language and replied, "Yes sir!"

I extricated myself from his grasp and ran out the front door, slamming it behind me. I ran down the stair well rather than the elevator, in order not to wait, so they couldn't chase me and out the door of Le Parker Meridien. I looked east then west and ran westward towards 7th Avenue and the subway. Even though I was only sixteen, I felt I needed to escape and felt confident enough to easily find my way back. I thought I should return to Greenwich Village as it could be fun. And somehow take my mind off of my dysfunctional family and brutal, uncompromising father, Maybe I might enjoy some Blitz Chess in Washington Square or maybe a coffee house seeing some folk music or poetry reading. But my mood was far from docile. I was infuriated and indignant at his total lack of understanding. The worse for me was those slaps. This was minor compared to his usual punishing beatings but nevertheless they enraged me. I felt a certain incomprehensible force that I couldn't elucidate or compare to anything I experienced previously.

I entered the club, sat and ordered coffee. I did encounter some startled and surprising gazes but did not react to them. After all, I was a young kid sitting in a Greenwich Village coffee house alone. I watched a poet recite a vague poem about equality:

Why do we not love each other?
Why is it right that we continue to hate each other?
Are we not all humans, black, white, yellow or brown?
Don't we all deserve the same existence?
How did we go so wrong?
The solution is love and understanding, not struggle.

I found her recital a bit juvenile, arcane and unsophisticated for presentation in a major NY coffee house, but I frankly I was in my own world and not mindful of the entire content or its completion. I looked at the other attendees in the audience and focused on a woman, thirty-something or possibly a bit older, who reminded me of my mother, with big brown eyes and wavy brown wavy, long hair as she passed the entrance of the club. She did not stop and hurried down the street. I ran out looked at her back as she walked briskly down the street. I don't know what possessed me or propelled me, but the urge was irrepressible. I kept hearing in my head: Go on, do it. I walked after her realizing that I needed to consummate this urge. I continued to follow her. I couldn't intelligently imagine what was driving me. I wondered how the thought about my mother was part of the underlying urge. Was it part of the equation? She reached Perry St. and turned unto it. I followed closely. I was sweating, my pulse was racing but my mind was blank beside the constant compulsion. I was breathing heavily with quick short breaths as I felt the excitement building. As she reached for the knob of the door to open the entrance, I hit her hard on the head. When I heard the gasp, I felt a strange sensation. I hit her again and dragged her to a nearby alley way. The terror in her eyes excited me further as I searched my jeans for the switchblade I had bought some time ago. She screamed freed her hands and scratched me on the side of my face. I muffled her mouth with a cloth handkerchief. She struggled ferociously but I was stronger, and it felt as though the adrenaline rush was impelling me. I removed the knife, clicked it open and slashed her throat. She panted and I slashed again and again and again. Blood was spurting from her neck, and I felt my first release and then removed her clothes and raped her.as she gasped. I watched her face as she died and finally realized what it was I was searching for. I realized that what I needed to do to keep me sane was to kill. I need to see terror and hurt in others to appease my own hurt. I needed to see terror in others to placate my own terror. I must have been daydreaming or in the middle of a nightmare because the look on her face and the terror it revealed jolted me to reality. I became breathless and screamed, which frightened Maria, lying at my side.

"Evan? Evan? Are you ok?"

"Uh. Yeah, Yeah, Bad dream I guess."

"A nightmare, I would say."

"Yeah. I guess so."

"Do you want to talk about it?"

"No, not really. I was just thinking about my parents: my father and his constant abuse and my mother's enabling it."

"Hey. You never spoke about them before. Are you sure you don't want to talk about is some more? It seems to have upset you considerably."

"No, Maria, I'd rather not. Can we please change the subject?"

I arose from the futon, put on my briefs, then my pants and my shirt and started to exit her room.

"Hey! Wait! Where are you going?" asked the sweet Maria. "Let's talk. I'm a good listener."

"You are sweet. I'm sure you are, but I better get back. This has been fun. Let's do it again, ok?"

"Are you sure? You can stay. My roommate is not coming back tonight."

"Oh, no. I can't but that is so kind of you, but I better go."

"Then, please call me tomorrow. I'd like to see you again."

"Sure," I said as I opened the door to depart.

The next morning, I had my first creative writing class with Prof. Bergman. I was very enthusiastic about this class. Prof Bergman was a known literary critic and had written some of the most scathing reviews of assorted well-known authors. I intended to be a writer and what better way to get indoctrinated than by this malevolent critic, who never published an original piece himself. He did nothing but criticize. Yet, this was exactly what I wanted: the critique. I wanted to be a respected writer and it was easy to imagine that if Bergman appreciated and respected you, the literary world would surely parrot his acceptance. I thought my writing was fairly mature and had received encouragement from my senior high school A.P. English teacher and from the faculty editor of the "Beaumont Buzz," the literary magazine that we published bimonthly. I had recently written an essay on global warming and the lack of an adequate current response by the government that was well received and sent to The Beaumont Gazette as an op-ed piece. In addition, I had written a short story that was published in the Boston Literary Magazine, called the "Quiet Teen," a semi-autobiographical expose of a lonely teenager, which shocked my parents and created quite a sensation in school because this lonely kid finally committed suicide, which unfortunately was unrecognized in Beaumont as an emerging health crisis in young people.

"Good morning! I'm Professor Paul Bergman and I will attempt to introduce you to the art of creative writing. This will take the form of a seminar and even though it is an introductory class, much is expected of you. The class will be difficult as I am very condemnatory of poor writing and will not hesitate to apprise you of lack of talent or writing ability and dissuade you from pursuing a career in the same. Are there any questions?"

He looked at the twenty students present found no hands or inquiries so he proceeded, "Although most of the assignments will be writing samples, I will assign you occasional pieces to review as examples of topics that will aid you in your course work but also hopefully in your future writing. Ok then. For next week, I'd like you to submit an example of your poetry. I've always found poetry as an excellent example of one's creative abilities. If you've never written poetry, you probably don't belong in this class. But let's see what we have here. Write one for this assignment. The syllabus is on my desk. As a point of emphasis, please note the final assignment is due before the holidays and is either a novella, less than one hundred pages, three short stories, or a screenplay, either an adaptation of a work of fiction or non-fiction or an original one."

I looked at the others and there seemed to be shock at the breadth of this assignment. But I was undeterred. As a matter of fact, I had already begun a treatment of an interesting novel, "Deadly Motivations", a medical thriller about a medical treatment for lymphoma using a prion, that is purloined by a terrorist organization and mutated to a dangerous form resulting in universal havoc-a pandemic casing severe illness, death and economic ruin for the global population.

"Again! Any questions? If not grab a copy of the syllabus on your way out and good luck."

The Innocence Project working with NYPD finally produced a DNA sample from the Captree slaying. There were tiny fragments of skin under Captree's wife's middle and forefinger of her right hand. The obvious anticipation was that it would prove Compton's innocence or at least lead to a new trial with evidence supporting same. The attorney for the Project was able to argue for a retrial with the new DNA evidence at hand.

Captree, who remained at the Walker throughout the two weeks it too to get results of the DNA sample time, had not heard from Compton or the "kidnappers" in the last few days, but was now hopeful of his daughter's return. He was ambivalent and despaired in the fact that Compton might be innocent, and his wife's rapist and murderer was still free. The thought unnerved him as this individual could very well kill or rape again. After a meeting with Saunders and Francis he walked back to the Walker and there she was.

Claudia came running to him, "Daddy, daddy."

"Claudia, are you ok? Did anyone hurt you? Can you tell me anything?"

"Not really. I was blindfolded the whole time, but I am not hurt and I'm fine. I am so frightened. It was terrible. I was in a dark room, without any contact. I was not allowed to watch television. I was given some children books for entertainment. They did feed me but only once a day with terrible tasting food. I kept asking for you, but they never talked to me. It was absolutely horrible, daddy. Do you have any idea what happened? Who did this and why?"

"We have an idea and we do know why you were released. I'm sorry. I can't give you any details, but it did concern your mom's death and probably the man who was in prison for it."

He hugged her and kissed her head and sighed, "Come let's go to the police station. I want to let them know you are safe. They'll probably want a statement from you."

"Can this happen again? I'm so frightened," she asked quaveringly.

Chapter 11

The workload at Columbia was a bitch. Between the reading assignments for the Core Curriculum, the other course load, and the writing assignments for Bergman, I was overwhelmed. My only diversion was Maria, who I saw on weekends, but unfortunately only occasionally. The weekend of Thanksgiving, I decided, to visit my parents. What a strange trip. We hardly spoke the entire time. Thanksgiving at my home was usually a low-key affair. But this year mom decided to invite her parents and sister with her significant other and a few neighbors. You can imagine how Thomas Dicks felt with this invasion of people that he hardly cared for and the tumult impinging on his "precious" time. I had mentioned previously that he was short tempered but with this multitude in his home he was worse than ever. I had to get out of there for my own sanity so I told them I would have to get back to NY by Saturday since I was working on a project that would be due in two weeks. Of course, my father was not dissatisfied with that pronouncement but was indignant about all the guests imposing on him and let my poor mother know it.

"What the fuck are you doing? Do I really need this shit? I bust my ass all week and come home to this dissonance. You really care very little about how I feel? Do you?"

"Come on, Tom. It's Thanksgiving and only a short weekend. We'll be back to normal before you know. Anyway, your son is home for the weekend. Aren't you pleased to see him?" she asked calmly.

"Oh, by the way I have to get back by Saturday. I'm working on a screenplay for my creative writing class. I'm doing a treatment of a novel that I recently read as a screenplay and it's due in two weeks," I repeated interrupting the argument. The disappointment my mother expressed was palpable. My father looked at her with disdain while shouting at me, "Go to hell you little shit!"

Hearing this, I retreated to my room to the solitude and loneliness of the room I had withdrawn to so many times before. I found solace in the dark and quiet and thought about my dysfunctional parents. Why did she always surrender to his belligerence? Why was she so impuissant and pathetic? She always just stood there with a poignant accepting look on her face as if to say, "Woe is me." Why didn't she just leave the bastard? Why did she always acquiesce? Her resigned attitude upset me and angered me to the point I began to blame her: for the dysfunction, for my father's anger and abuse and, my God, my own murderous psyche. This was an easy transference that I found gratifying. Take out my rage and weakness of my mother on others. Too simple? I thought. I wondered about the other explanations and analyses, but I probably would need the help of a psychiatrist to truly understand. I reclined on my bed closed my eyes and began to feel the urge, the sensation, the need.

I boarded the Amtrak at North Station in Boston at 1pm on that Saturday. I chose a window seat in coach in a mostly empty car and powered on my laptop. I thought I would try to get some work done on my screenplay, but it was hopeless. I was too angry and upset to accomplish anything. As I stared out the window, I kept the resentment for my father and the empathy for my mother fresh in my mind, while I daydreamed of previous times of harmony. I thought about our "family" times, vacations on cruises to Alaska, St. Petersburg and Norway or visiting Walt Disney World, all when I was much younger. I couldn't comprehend when it all went wrong. What changed him? After a short respite, I stopped thinking about it and returned to my manuscript. The screenplay for "Deadly Motivations" was nearing completion. I was proud of the effort and thought that it was meritorious and was hoping that Bergman thought so also. As I completed an especially climactic scene, I felt a presence near me. Looking up from my laptop, I noticed a youngish woman on my left. She was in her early twenties, not very attractive but not homely either. I thought, I hope she doesn't start a conversation as I'd rather work on this manuscript. But she disappointed me by starting a conversation immediately.

"Hey, I'm Jen. Who are you?"

"Huh?"

"I'm sorry. I have a long train ride and thought you'd like to schmooze."

"Shmooze?"

"Uh, uh. Well, this train is heading to New York so I thought you might understand local lingo. It's a Yiddish word for talk, you know, senseless conversation."

"Oh yeah. I'm sorry. I'm kind of busy. I have a deadline on this manuscript."

"Deadline? Are you a journalist or something?"

"No! I'm a freshman at Columbia and working on a creative writing assignment."

She looked at me and said, "Wow. Smart kid, huh? Well anyway, I apologize. I won't bother you any further."

Feeling miscreant I replied, "Hey, I'm sorry for acting like an ass. I don't mean any disrespect. My name is Evan."

She smiled, "No worries, dear. Just making conversation. Don't concern yourself. You didn't insult me at all."

I looked at her and suddenly felt my anger at my father, my disappointment and sympathy for my mother and my own weird feeling of needing release. My personality suddenly completed changed as I was again beckoning the monster within.

"Hey, how about some coffee on me?" I said pleasantly voicing that inner being.

She smiled again and winked, "Sure," she said.

I don't know why but this infuriated me. I again felt compelled by an inexplicable driving force. We spoke a while longer and as the train approached NY, we went to the dining car. Having coffee and a sandwich, we sat in the dining car as the train headed into White Plains. When the train pulled into the station, she politely excused herself to go to the restroom. Suddenly, it hit me, that urge that indescribable sensation, that unstoppable feeling and need. I followed her. She opened the door and I slammed her into the approximate nine square foot cubicle, with barely room to turn. Staring into her terrified face, I remained silent while I muffled her mouth. The look on her face was clearly the one I was looking for and savored. Her muffled cries excited me. I removed my knife, clicked open the switch blade and perceived her mouthing, "No, No, No." Yes, this is exactly what I need. Yes. Feeling my release as I slashed her throat, I removed her clothes and raped her as she gasped with her final breaths. Calmly I washed my face and hands. Then I proceeded to cut her chest at her heart with the "cross". I looked at her again, shuddered while I waited for the train to pull into Penn Station. I left the rest room, locked the door behind me and went to my seat to get my laptop and knapsack. I sneaked into the rush of people leaving the train and then integrated myself into the swarm of humanity at Penn Station even on a Saturday. I left the station on 8th Avenue and hailed a cab for the ten-mile ride to Columbia. When I reached the dorm, I flopped down on my bed and began feeling the usual post –killing remorse. This fascinated me. In trying to explain my actions, it was hard to rationalize the dichotomy.

After working all of Sunday, I completed the manuscript. By Monday morning's creative writing class, the completed manuscript seemed ready, and I handed it to Bergman, who registered surprise at the punctuality of the submission.

"Hey. Good job, Dicks. A screenplay, huh? and early? Hmm "Deadly Motivations"?

"Yes sir? It's a recent book I found online. It's a medical mystery. It's quite interesting and very timely. It's written by a physician. I thought it would make a fascinating movie or even a limited television series. I sure hope you like it. "

That day the class dragged as I was very anxious to see Maria, who had returned to campus that morning. We met on the steps of Lowe Library. We kissed and hugged. I related my disastrous

Thanksgiving weekend as she listened attentively to my tales of "woe". She responded with condolences, but I subconsciously questioned her sincerity. Although I probably shouldn't have, I mentioned her disingenuous tone. But she responded with another kiss and hug and stated, "At least your family celebrates Thanksgiving. My family all worked. They have no time or money to have a Thanksgiving dinner or a celebration."

I looked into her forlorn, sorrowful eyes and hugged her. "I am so sorry. I had never really asked you about your family or origins or even where you live. I am such a dumb shit, inconsiderate, thoughtless in addition to self-centered. Please forgive me."

"That's really quite alright. You're sweet and I accept your apology."

"Thanks. You're great. I've never met anyone like you. You're so self- deprecating and yet beautiful, brilliant and kind."

"Here's my story. I live in Queens in Elmont. My parents come from Ecuador and arrived in the US about eight years ago when I was ten. My parents are illegal immigrants, and I am one of the so-called "Dreamers". My father is a laborer and works whenever a job presents itself and my mom works as a domestic. She cleans homes in Jamaica Estates or Forest Hills. She works daily in as many homes as she can, cleans, cooks, shops and takes care of families. She doesn't have a single family employer as it is difficult to find one home to work at without proper papers unless the employer is willing to chance getting caught and my mother being deported.

"Your family must be under constant fear during the Trump administration with ICE actively trying to deport all illegal immigrants."

"I can't begin to tell you the constant fear and trepidation we live. Hopefully it will get somewhat better after he leaves. But there is always that underlying consternation of being discovered and sent back to Ecuador. At least the Supreme Court has blocked any deportation of the "dreamers: When we arrived in the States, I didn't speak much English. But that dramatically changed once I started kindergarten. I did grow up streetwise and learned some conversational English in those streets. My neighborhood was and remains a most disconcerting shit hole. There are tenements and low-income projects, where most live surrounded by burnt out store fronts. The park or playground is a drug infested marketplace for cocaine, heroin, fentanyl, or OxyContin® with the occasional barbiturate thrown in. MS-13, the infamous LA gang that is El Salvador based and now international is ever present in Queens and Elmont is no exception. My brother was killed in gang crossfire when he was seven, while walking home from school with my dad. You can only imagine the devastation that caused my family. As a result, my dad threated to take us out of NY, but it was hard to do given the limitations of our immigration circumstances. Once I entered school I gravitated to the more stable group of Latinos, although easier said than done. Slowly, I found a cadre of friends that was somewhat more mixed with occasional Latinos but also Indians, Pakistanis and Africans. Obviously, the diversity of the population of my neighborhood is evident. This gave me a tremendous understanding of varying races, peoples, attitudes and cultures. It also introduced me to those that care about education and foster it in their families as my parents had done. It shaped my sociology and thoughts. I excelled in math and science and naturally wanted to pursue that as a career but my attitude towards inequality, racial injustices and cultural bias started shaping my future toward a different direction. I thought I wanted to serve the community and my people and therefore, I intended to go to law school and try to help the indigent. Bu my love for music and the English language is driving me in a different direction. So, I guess overall, I am still undecided about my future. But I presume it is easy for you to see when you speak about a stable family with Thanksgiving dinner and a steady environment, no matter how dysfunctional, it raises my exasperation. I never knew that stability or that commitment. I was disenchanted and now still continue to search for that. I can only imagine what your family dysfunction is like for you, and I do indeed commiserate with you. But please don't think you have a monopoly on sadness, indignation and despondency. My family is hardly as flawed but just as unhappy and hurt. Anyway, let's not fight about it and make up and go on without bad feelings or grudges. Okay?"

"Shit. What a story. I obviously had no idea and should have been more thoughtful and understanding. I should have assumed that your story was a tough one."

"Why because my name is Maria Lopez and I have brown skin?"

"No. No Maria. Hmm…Yeah, I guess that is it and once again the inherent racism of white folk emerges. Please again forgive me. I think very highly of you and would very much like to continue our relationship. Please don't let this discussion have a bearing on it or deleterious effect. Please."

"No worries, dear Evan. You're a good guy and I like you very much. What would one expect from a privileged white dude form a lily-white suburb? You did say you come from some neighborhood outside of Boston, right? Tell me more."

"Hey."

"Kidding. Come on tell me your story," she inquired.

"Well, What can I say? Yes, I come from Beaumont, Mass., a lily-white suburb of Boston. Three families of color reside in the entire town. My mother went to Wellesley and is a sociologist with an MA in analytics, who did teach for a while at Tufts University and took a position with a research firm analyzing data on global pandemics. Currently she works part-time remotely to spend more time with my brother, James who just started high school. I think she did mention that now that James is in high school, she'll probably return to full time analytic work. Interestingly, she recently was offered a gig analyzing data for the New England Patriots.

"Wow. That sounds like a fun job," she interjected.

"My father is an electrical engineer, but he is a partner in a hedge fund. Unfortunately, this wealth and power has created a monster. He is intolerant of the "simple folk". He treats my mom with condescension. His insolences and impertinence are shameful. He also has abused James and me both mentally and physically. Yet, she continues to accede. She never takes him to task for this abuse. I have considered calling child services with a complaint. But she always has stopped me. I don't understand what the magical magnetism is that propels her assent, but it's there, nonetheless. Sometimes, I wonder whether she'll leave as soon as James completes high school. It makes me crazy. I walk around with this profound anger which feels unsettled. Recently I even, started blaming my mom for his abuse because she doesn't confront him. Is that crazy or what?"

"Hey, it's obviously a very difficult situation. She is compromising but it seems at your detriment. I think you probably should report him. Does James have similar feelings?"

"I'm not sure. Unfortunately, I never confronted him about it. I've mostly kept things to myself."

I continued with my history, "I went to the public high school, which is obviously a high-achieving one with off the charts competitiveness. Every parent in that community wants only one thing for their "brilliant" child, the Ivy League: Harvard, Yale or Princeton."

Laughingly she added, "What about Columbia?"

"Lower tier and second rate," I added snickering. "As a matter of fact, I was accepted to the NYU Scholar's Program with a free ride and a guarantee into the Tisch School of the Arts. I can't begin to tell you the fireworks that that conversation created."

"You dad sounds like a real bastard. Boy I can imagine how he would feel about his son seeing an Ecuadorian "dreamer."

"Don't ask. Have you heard enough about the dysfunctional Dicks existence?"

"Well, actually I would like to hear more about you and your family especially about your deep seeded feelings. They sound disturbing."

I looked at her quizzically, "Disturbing?"

She understood my disquiet at describing my feelings as disturbing. "Hey, I'm sorry, I didn't mean disturbing. I meant plausible."

"Those are opposites. What did you really mean? You think I'm a psycho or something!" I said angrily.

"Hey, hey. I didn't say that. I just meant your feelings seemed very strong and I wanted to explore them further with you. Maybe I could help to allay that tension and anger?"

"Yeah. Right? Look at the shrink?"

"Hey. Come on. We haven't seen each in other since Wednesday. Come on and lighten up, will ya?" she said as she grabbed my neck pulled me to her and kissed me flush on the mouth. Feeling her tongue explore my moth, I pulled away.

"No!"

"What is it?" she repeated as she tried to appease my indignation at that very unsettling comment. "I'm sorry. I didn't mean anything by it. Please believe me"

I looked at her, thought further about her rectitude and decency and thought her honorable and so I returned her kiss.

"That's the Evan I remember. Now let's go back to your room. Is your roomie in?"

"No. He gets back later tonight."

"Great", Maria said with a sly, evil, welcoming look on her face. But I couldn't forget what she had said, their meaning and implications and the effect it could have on our relationship. But that would have to await a later time.

I grabbed her hand and pulled her toward my dorm.

The rest of the semester passed uneventfully. My grades were okay with two A's and two B's. As I was starting to pack for a trip home for the holidays, I received a most unexpected e-mail form Prof. Bergman: *Hey Dicks. Read your treatment of Deadly Motivations and think it's fascinating. It is well written, and I believe you're right it has tremendous potential would like to talk about it. Please come by my office today at twelve.* I responded immediately with excitement: *Thank you. See you at twelve.*

I couldn't wait for the two hours to pass. As I continued to pack my knap sack, I kept thinking. What does he mean fascinating? The word potential really excited me. What is he interested in? Before I ran to his office, I called Maria to let her know.

"Hey, Bergman liked my screenplay and wants to talk."

"What do you think?"

"I have no idea, but he obviously knows a bunch of people in the entertainment world and knows "everyone", who could make something happen with this. I'll let you know."

"Hey. Good luck."

"Thanks. I'll talk to you later."

I walked up the flight of stairs to his office at 11:55am and noticed the empty anteroom without a secretary present so I knocked on the closed door and impatiently waited.

"Come in," said the voce from behind the door. His office was a cluttered mess. His desk was piled high with papers, books, pencils, pens, and a discarded coffee cup. Bergman was sitting behind a stack of blue books (exams I gathered) and noticed me out of the corner of his eye.

"Afternoon, Dicks. Is it afternoon?"

"Yes, it is, sir," I told the absent-minded professor.

"Well, that is quite a manuscript you handed in. Where did you say you got the source material?"

"I've always been interested in medical mysteries, so I keep my eye out for new works and found this one on Amazon. I saw a pretty positive review and noticed it was written by a physician, so I bought the Kindle version. Reading it, I found the subject fascinating especially given the involvement of a bio-terrorist group and a pandemic. I felt it lent itself to a possible screenplay or teleplay. Your assignment just played right into my vision."

"Yes. I'm not sure about its commercial value but I have to tell you the writing is superb. For a young author, your certainly do have maturity. The synthesis of plot within the context of a screenplay was excellent. I also do think the plot is intriguing especially in face of the threats of pandemics and bioterrorism that seem to be ever present. I always wondered what the possible confluence of the two, a bio-terrorist group using a pandemic as a tool would look like. This is surely a start."

"I agree. That's what attracted me to the work, too. I thought about calling the author to discuss it further. He's a physician who wrote the novel under a pseudonym, J. Paul Bradley. He works in New York, but I haven't gotten the chance to call."

"I think you might have to legally call him. You have to get the rights to the book."

"The rights, sir?"

"Yes. Shit. I almost forgot what I called you about. By the way, I gave your manuscript an "A.""

"Thank you, sir."

"Anyway. I'm sending it to a content editor I know at Netflix."

"Netflix?" I said excitedly.

"Yes, indeed. I want to see what he thinks about the potential for this work as a film or possibly a series."

"Film? Series????"

"Are you having trouble hearing, Dicks?"

"No, sir. I'm just so surprised and excited. That's all."

"Well. Jesus. You should fucking be. I never do this for a student. But I just think that this is exceptional."

"Thank you, sir. Thank you."

"Ok. I'm busy. I'll call you if I hear anything. By the way if they like it, it may mean having to transfer to a school in Los Angeles. But I don't think that would be an issue for you, right?"

"No sir."

At 2:15pm, The Northeast Corridor train was ready to leave for the Newark Airport Station. As of yet, no one had inspected the restrooms. At 2:22pm, a woman with a three-year-old curly blonde-haired, blue-eyed daughter with a cherubic happy face were seated two rows behind the exit. Mom was getting settled, when her daughter mentioned that she had to go sissy. "Already? We just got on the train."

The daughter insisted so mom grabbed her hand and proceeded to the nearest rest room. Pushing the door open she witnessed the carnage. She quickly hid her blond surprised child and screamed. "My

God! Help me! Someone help me. Oh! My God. Come sweetie let's go. We'll find another bathroom." Hearing her screams multiple passengers came running to where she was and discovered the dead and bloodied Jen. There was blood all over the floor, sink and ceiling. Her dead body lay still on the floor with her legs draped on the commode. The conductor was summoned, and he alerted the engineer. They were in the tunnel under the Hudson River by this time, so they proceeded to the next station at Newark Airport. A silent anxious hush prevailed over the car on the seven-minute trip to the station. Awaiting the train's arrival were the NY-NJ Transit Police and two Newark detectives. When they entered the tiny cubicle, they were shocked at the scene. They proceeded to the mother and daughter, who were surrounded by the passengers and tried to calm them down, especially the mother with her daughter. The crime investigation team were already at work, by the time Saunders and Francis arrived. They had been summoned by the NJ detectives as the crime had obviously been perpetrated in their jurisdiction. They looked at the body with the very prominent cross etched on the victim's chest and knew exactly that the Mass-NY rapist /killer had struck again. The Crime Investigation team took samples as the two New York detectives interviewed the surrounding passengers.

"You discovered the body, didn't you?" Saunders asked the mother, while her daughter kept crying and repeating over and over again, "I have to sissy, mommy, please."

"Yes," replied the mother. "Please excuse me while I take care of her."

"Of course."

Upon her return, they continued to question her, but she had very little to offer. No one saw the victim enter the bathroom or anyone follow her in, and no one saw anyone leave that bathroom. The spent the next three hours questioning every passenger but this proved to be fruitless. They deduced that the killer must have exited in NY. They also discovered that the victim had entered the train in New Haven and was on her way to Philadelphia. They would have to interview her parents and her acquaintances there but that would have to wait. The fact the train emanated from the Boston North Station was of interest to them in light of the previous killings. They would have to review the entire passenger list of those who started in Boston with a ticket to NY. That should narrow down the possibilities somewhat, they thought to themselves laughingly. Following the three-hour delay for the interviews, the CSI and the removal of the body, the train started afresh to its destination but to the obvious dismay and chagrin of the passengers. According to the Amtrak representative summoned, they could do nothing but apologize and reimburse for a future ticket.

"Well, we'll have lots of DNA to work with now, don't you think?" Francis said to Saunders.

"I guess. I did see semen on the poor lady's leg. What a horror show. This guy is clearly a psychopath and dangerous and I really believe we have to find him fast to prevent other killing but also to circumvent a public maelstrom created by the press. We're going to have to admit to them that this looks like a serial killer, which can very well panic the entire city. What a fucking mess!"

Saunders thought it a good idea to call Captree for multiple reasons: To see whether anything came of the investigation into the head count of possible Beaumont students at Columbia, to let him know about the recent murder and to ask him to check the trains from Boston and passengers on the same and their home addresses and whether anyone had purchased a ticket from Beaumont. In addition, she wanted to check in with him as she really enjoyed talking to him and being with him and even make some excuse to possibly sneak up to Beaumont for a visit.

It didn't take long for the press to learn of the Amtrak event and publicize it over multimedia exposure. The harrowing details of the grisly murder resulted in the hysterical response as predicted by Saunders.

TVs around the metropolitan area blared the story: **Breaking New: Serial Killer is at large.** The details described the murder on the Amtrak train headed for Washington D.C. It mentioned the specific details of the methodology including the cross branding on the left chest. This heightened the suspicion that this indeed was a serial murderer and suddenly panic was evident. The conversation on most people's lips was exactly that: **"Who will be next? Is anyone safe?"** This was a dubious issue as it was clear that the profile of the victims was that of a young woman of no specific background or occupation. There was no clear-cut pattern as to motive either. But the cross remained mysterious. Was it an indication of a religious fanatic who was obsessed with licentious vamps? That probably was true for at least one of the victims, the prostitute in the village, Johanna Morrissey, her real name. When Captree heard the most recent report, he immediately thought about that possibility and the reaction it would garner from Emily's father and he let Saunders know on the phone call. She mentioned this to Francis and their profile now included a religious zealot, who preyed on dissolute women. Saunders had seen this profile many times previously and could summarize a probable psychological profile, which might be able to narrow the search especially since the first victim was from a small town with a limited population.

Chapter 12

I returned home for the semester break with ambivalent anticipation of what my parents would say about the December events that changed my whole world. My transfer request to USC was granted for the USC film school with little difficulty. Dr. Bergman had spoken to Prof Daley, the dean of the USC School of Cinematic Arts (SCA) and they admitted me to the undergraduate screenwriting program. I was ecstatic. I never dreamed I would advance this rapidly with a potential writing career. Now I had to face my parents. I broached the subject with great trepidation on the night I returned as we sat down to dinner late. My father was always late claiming job responsibilities.

"M -Mom, D-dad, I have something to discuss. You know that I intend to be writer, right? Well, I handed in a paper to my creative writing class, of a screenplay treatment of a book I had been reading. My professor loved it and sent it to a content editor at Netflix. Anyway, he loves my writing and the screenplay and suggested I'd be wasting time at Columbia and should go to a film school. He suggested my potential is enormous. He called the dean at the USC School of Cinematic Arts also known as SCA and pulled some strings and they admitted me. So, I'll be transferring to USC starting in the spring semester." I sat there waiting for the expected fallout and shit that came like a nuclear reaction.

Tom Dicks was furious. "What the hell are you talking about? Film school my ass. You're not transferring to any fucking Los Angeles film school. You hear me?" His screams were so loud they frightened poor James. My mom was a bit more empathetic but negative, nonetheless.

"Wow, Evan, that is so fantastic. I am so proud of you, but you're too young to pursue such an unknown with an unpredictable reputation. Why not wait for graduate school and see where this writing passion goes? I really think that both of us will be amenable to waiting, making sure this is real and following that course after you graduate from Columbia."

"I don't think so. This is my future, and this is what I want to do with my life and the quicker I start the better it is, I'm old enough to make my own decisions."

"Oh yeah, you little shit and who in hell is going to support you?"

"I got a scholarship with a full ride, and I'll get a part-time job for expenses. Anyway, maybe the manuscript that Dr. Bergman sent to Netflix will sell."

"I fucking can't believe this crap. Sarah, tell him he can't go. I forbid it."

"Sorry, Father Dicks, I don't need you goddam permission. You know, in addition to

beating the shit out of me constantly, you never supported me or even cared about me so fuck you."

"Evan!!!"

"Sorry mom, it's time you realized who you are married to and what kind of human being this is. Have a nice dinner." With that statement, I arose grabbed my bag that was still packed and stormed out the door hearing my mom cry out, "Evan, Evan, please!"

I heard my mom come running after me, but I had nothing further to say to her. I was heading for the train to Boston and then back to New York and although she tried, she couldn't stop me. My father never even bothered. I had decided that if the scenario I envisioned played out this way. I would spend the next few days with Maria and then go to LA. In spite of the sorrow of my mom and her obvious hurt and disappointment, this was something I had to do. Anyway, she defended that child molester without compunction and with disregard of my being and safety.

Maria was very welcoming as was the Lopez family. It was apparent that the squalor she described was hardly an exaggeration. She lived in a fourth-floor walk-up, which seemed extraordinarily strenuous for her mother, who had obvious arthritis. She was an elderly appearing bent woman with a pleasant disposition, accommodating and gracious. Her dad was a tall, noble appearing, man of fifty-five or so with a strong square chin, black wavy hair, brown piercing eyes and a pleasant manner. This was so fascinating to me. This poor family who lived paycheck to paycheck never seemed to complain, which was diametrically opposite of my affluent, upscale family, who constantly discussed their misery and unhappiness. I found this hard to comprehend or justify. But maybe just maybe this was why I am the way I am. Garnering the necessary love and respect from your parents is essential to a healthy psyche. Was it not Freud who preached that aggressive behavior is derived? The third stage of psychological development is the phallic stage. During this third stage of psychologic development, the so-called phallic stage (at approximately three to six years of age) when the focus of the developing psyche is on the genitalia and, initially, on the parent of the opposite sex. This can only be resolved if the developing mind eliminates the opposite sex and identifies with the same sex. If this did not occur one could turn to aggression? I debated this with myself. If this were true, why am I so harmful to women? Maybe I am trying to get back at my father by harming women (my mother). I laughed at myself and the psychobabble that was floating in my mind. But I do hate my father and do disrespect my mother for not defending me and even herself.

The Lopez's only had a three-bedroom apartment, so I slept on the couch. Our dinner discussion centered on Columbia and the pride they felt for Maria, I agreed and told her parents that she was one of the smartest and nicest people I have yet to meet at Columbia.

Elizabeth, Maria's mother said in her broken English, "Evan, Maria says that you are the brightest student at school."

"Mama Sita. No, I didn't. I said one of the brightest that I have met. "Muy diferente."

"Ah. Perdoneme."

"No Worries. I know I'm not the smartest kid in school."

Maris also said that you are moving to Los Angeles.
"Yes, I am."

"You go to school there?"

"Yes, to the University of Southern California to study making movies. Understand?"

"Si, Si."

After we dined of arroz con pollo, Maria and I went down to take a walk on Linden Blvd. Suddenly Maria stopped grabbed my arm and said, "I can't believe you're leaving. I only just met you and grown very fond of you."

"And I you, but this is a once in a lifetime opportunity."

"I guess but isn't Columbia a much better institution than USC. Don't you think the prestige of Columbia would carry more weight than even SCA?"

"Maria, to tell you the truth. Part of the reason I'm leaving is to get as far away from my shitty home life and family especially that son of bitch father of mine and his obsequious wife."

She turned to me grabbed my chin and kissed me passionately and said, "Tal vez. I'll join you."

"Tal vez?"

"Maybe."

"My God. That would be great."

Lifting her chin and gazing into her soulful eyes, I wondered why in the back recesses of my mind did I not want to harm this girl. Was it her apparent devotion to me or was it her sweet innocence, or was it the fact that she was in most respects the exact opposite of me? She came from immigrant parents; she was a woman of color with Spanish as her first language and dirt poor or was it only the timing and that eventually my urge will overcome me and I will want to harm her and I will want to experience the same sensation as the with the others: that feeling of release when I observed the terror and fear in the victims' eyes. That feeling of overcoming the victim and displaying that power that I sought. Yes. maybe. Yes, maybe when she visits me in California if she does. Maybe that is when that overwhelming urge will overcome my current suppressive id. I obviously didn't say a word or act differently. I kissed her and again said, "You must come. You absolutely must come because I very much know how much I will miss you if you don't.

"Yes, Evan, yes I will definitely come."

"Great, Maria."

I kissed her again before we walked back to her parents' apartment.

I left the next morning and reached JFK by 8am. For unknown reasons, guilt overtook me, and I called home.

"Hey, mom it's Evan."

"Evan, where are you? What are you doing? Come home!"

"One question at a time, mom, please. I'm at JFK and ready to get on a flight to LA. I start school in a few weeks at USC. My professor was kind enough to help me get in and get a scholarship. No, I'm not coming home, and I am not going to speak to that bastard again. I really think you should take James and leave him, too. Undoubtedly, he'll hurt you or James or both of you soon. I'm really afraid for you."

"Evan, please don't say that. He's your father and he loves you very much. He even told me so the night you left. He wants you to return and try to make amends and work things out. Please, Evan."

"Bullfuckingshit! He's lying and trying to ingratiate himself to you. Can't you see his duplicity? He may actually love me, but his anger is too easily provoked to an unmanageable extent, where it is impossible for me to stay there. Anyway, I have this unprecedented transformational opportunity to create and learn and pursue a career that is preternatural. I'm sorry."

"No, Evan, No. Don't hang up, please."

"Sorry, mom."

"Will I hear from you again when you reach L.A?" I heard her say with a perceptible sob in her voice.

"I don't know."

I then hung up.

PART TWO
LOS ANGELES

*Two souls, alas, are housed within my breast, And
each will wrestle for the mastery there.*
-Johan Wolfgang Von Goethe (Faust)

Chapter 13

I boarded the American nonstop to Los Angeles at 8:52am and sat in Row 22 seat A, preparing for the six-hour flight to LAX. As I settled into the window seat, a middle aged bald professorial appearing man sat next to me in seat B. I really hoped he wasn't interested in me and didn't want to discuss the time of day, the Yankees losing streak, politics or climate change. I really wanted to remain anonymous on this flight and not discuss my plans, intentions, likes or dislikes. Boy was I wrong. Not a minute after liftoff, the questions started and didn't cease. Fortuitously, it turned out this gentleman had a PhD in comparative literature and taught at UCLA. In addition, he knew Bergman very well. I guess you can imagine what this six-hour flight turned out to be. It was a perpetual discussion of UCLA vs. USC, literature and the merits of English literature versus American literature. But to be totally honest when I mentioned going to SCA to the screenwriting program and my treatment of a novel, he was enthralled. He thought I was way too young to have garnered this amount of respect from someone as influential as Bergman. We discussed the novel and my perceived way of filming it, which seemed to entertain him and captivate him. I must confess, I was surprised but pleasantly pleased at his interest almost to the point of not believing him, thinking him disingenuous as if he was plant to encourage me. But who could have known I would be on this particular flight? Thus, finding this thought completed improbable, I continued my discussion and continued to delight in his response. As you probably can surmount, the six hours of this supposed boring flight passed fairly speedily. Upon landing, we gathered our bags and he said, "Evan, it has been a pleasure meeting such a fine intelligent and accomplished teenager. You must give me a call when you're settled. We can do dinner or lunch and maybe I can help this thing along."

I looked at him quizzically and thanked him. At which he conceded, "No, I'm serious. Don't you think that an English professor at UCLA knows many important people in the film industry. Well, if you doubt it, you're absolutely wrong. I indeed can be of assistance."

"So. sorry. I surely don't mean any disrespect. I was only surprised that you'd be willing to help a total stranger, who might have just dropped a load of bull shit on you that you might not know if true or not."

His obvious surprised face at my language was precious and gave me an unexpected triumphant jolt.

"Hey, I guess you haven't spoken to many teenagers recently. I'm joshing you. Yes, I do appreciate your offer and will definitely call when I'm settled at USC. I'll let Dr. Bergman know we spoke also." Leaving the plane, I took his business card:

Monroe Steinfeld, PhD
Professor of Comparative Literature
UCLA
Renee and David Kaplan Hall
Los Angeles, CA 90095

I took public transportation from the airport, the LAX FlyAway bus service to Union Station and a train to the USC campus. I checked in at Student Housing, the next morning after spending the night at the USC hotel. The admissions office had said I could check into the dorms early. I received my key and slowly proceeded to my room. It was still two weeks until classes would commence. Thus, I inquired from Student Resources about the possibility of part-time employment, to which they demurred. But luckily, the Daily Trojan listed a possibility at the

USC library-Doheny Memorial Library for a part-time clerk, sorter and data manager. Fortunately, the previous work-study student had left school early, and I was able to start the next day at twenty dollars an hour. How lucky can one get? Not only will I have spending money, but I'll get to meet lots of students. I told the administrator that I could work full-time for the next two weeks until classes started and would then give her my schedule for the rest of the semester. I thanked her profusely and walked out with unmitigated jubilance. Not only was I in LA, on my own, ready to translate my treatment of an obscure novel into a possible Netflix Original Series or film but I was at the best film school in the world, settled with a part-time job that could afford me the independence I sought. I waked back to Student Housing. I stopped, looked at the gorgeous campus and sat on Pardee Lawn, the main knoll outside of the Student Housing Administration building. This is just too perfect to imagine. A black thought suddenly entered my mind. Yes, but what about those feelings. Are you really ready to cease? Isn't that void still there? Don't you need to act on it soon if not immediately. I sat shuddering, fearful of my own being and what it could do. I closed my eyes and tried to think away the evil. But it was useless. I reopened my eyes looked at the cloudless blue sky. It was sixty-five degrees Fahrenheit in the middle of January. My mind will not detract from this. No, I will check these evil thoughts. Again, I thought:

How? Is it possible? Do I have control? Can I gain control? Never did I imagine the repercussions of my previous actions. I never perceived getting caught or going to jail. I never even realized the possibility. I had already killed four people over the past two or so years. Wasn't I a wanted criminal? Weren't they looking for the murderer? I remained there as if in a in a trance.

Suddenly I sensed someone standing over me. She was a California girl-blonde, blue eyed with straight hair to her mid back that was now falling over my face as she stared down at me.

"Hey, what you doing, man?"

"Lying here and dreaming. What are you doin?"

"Bending down and staring at this young guy in the middle of the lawn, who seems out of it."

"Wrong. I am not stoned. I just arrived from New York and kind of tired so I'm only resting."

"Bullshit", she exclaimed. "Let's share your shit. I could use a hit."

"Honestly, sister," I said as I bolted up right to emphasize my point.

"Ok. Ok. I'm sorry. I'm Samantha. But you can call me Sam. Everybody else does."

"Well, well. It's nice to meet you. I'm Evan."

"From New Yaalk?"

"No, Evan Dicks from Massachusetts.

"But you said?"

"I arrived from New York but I'm from Mass."

"Complicated, huh?" she said as she sat down next to me.

"Not really. I went to school at Columbia and just transferred to USC starting this semester," I explained eliminating much of the details.

"Smart guy, huh?"

"Not really."

"Well, I'm California, born and bred as you probably surmised."

"How so?"

"Well let's see, the long, blonde hair, the blue eyes, the cool accent and demeanor and the lack of reticence or timorousness. In addition, I guess the mucho athletic bod."

"Wow. Confidence surely without diffidence."

"Don't use those hundred-dollar words with me. You don't impress me."

"What the fuck you just rattled off timorousness and reticence and I'm using hundred-dollar words. Boy, you are a cool chick."

"That's what I said, bro."

"Why did you stop?" I asked looking into that beautiful well sculpted face with high cheek bones short upsloping nose and big slightly slanted blue eyes.

"I saw a cute guy and had nothing else going at the time."

"Thanks for nothing, Sam."

"Don't mention it hon. Hey, you wanna get some breakfast, lunch, whatever. I know a nice café nearby."

"Still have nothing else going now?" I asked facetiously.

"Not really," she said as she arose grabbing my hand. "I like New Yaaalk guys, and you are cute but not sure about how reliable or truthful you are. You've been bullshitting me now for the past thirty minutes."

"No. I have not. I am from Mass and did go to school at Columbia."

"No, you ass. I'm talking about being stoned."

I looked into those gorgeous cerulean eyes nearly melting and exclaimed, "I am absolutely without any bit of falsehood or dishonesty," as I placed my hand on my heart for emphasis.

Arising she grabbed my hand and pulled me up, "Let's go New Yaalk. Come on. I'm famished."

"Now. You're the one that sounds stoned."

We laughed as we walked hand in hand toward the campus exit. I thought. Boy, these California girls are everything everyone says they are. We proceeded about half mile on Trousdale Blvd to a local coffee shop, whose name had "Bean" something in it, but I can't remember it precisely nor it is important. We sat near the window. It was counter service, so I ordered a chocolate croissant with a cappuccino, low fat. She ordered a coffee Americano with a ham and cheese sandwich. The crowd in the shop was mostly representative of a college clientele with the exception of an occasional cop and construction worker. Our conversation was mostly surrounded school. She was a USC freshman studying psychology and hoping to get a PhD and becoming a clinical psychologist. She was interested in child psychology and the effect of child abuse. I then related my own story more fully mentioning the treatment of "Deadly Motivations", which, of course, she hadn't read, Prof Bergman, the film school and my interests in screen writing. I also mentioned Netflix although I felt it was too premature to discuss. Our conversation was animated and easy flowing and I felt at ease with her. She asked about girlfriends, and I did mention Maria. But qualified the response with "But I'm now in LA". She smiled that radiant sunshine smile and I was hooked. We stayed close to two hours when she excused herself and left for the bathroom. When she returned, she again grabbed my hand and said, "Let's go."

"Where to if I may ask."

"You'll see."

"Uh nah. I'm afraid of you with that athletic bod."

"Not to worry. I'm harmless." I followed her out the door chasing after her as she ran back toward campus.

"Hold up. I can't keep up."

She turned and laughed, "Then you will be left behind and miss the fun."

At that, I sped up and ran with her to the campus and her dorm.

"Samantha" by Clint Black played on the phone, but no one answered. At the other end of the line, the caller, a forty-eight-year-old blonde (dyed) suburban housewife was perplexed. Why, she thought, would she not answer? Two hours later, she tried again but again no response. Now she began to worry. She knew her daughter was fun-loving and irresponsible, but she had promised to be home for her sister's birthday dinner. When her husband arrived, she ran to him in a frenzy, with trepidation, "I haven't been able to reach Sam all day. She went to school today for some last-minute straightening at the dorm. She had promised to be home in time for Robin's dinner, but she hasn't responded to my numerous phone calls since one. What should we do? I'm frightened."

"Hey relax. You know how she is. She probably met some friends and lost track of the time or Robin's birthday."

"Yeah. I guess you're right." She then yelled out in a loud voice pointing to the upstairs where the bedrooms were, "Robin! Get ready. Our reservation at La Boheme is in an hour."

"Ok, Mom."

They left for La Boheme located halfway between Malibu and L.A. on the coast. The celebration was muted given the missing eldest daughter, but the food was delicious, and they enjoyed it despite. But the fear was pervasive and threatening at something being amiss. Multiple phone calls and messages were met without response. Now both parents were concerned. The drive back to their home was in ghost-like silence without conversation except for the continued dialing of Samantha's number with no response. They reached home at 9pm and Mrs. Joyce Clark wanted to call the police but her husband, Edward objected, stating that the cops wouldn't do anything until she was missing at least twenty-four hours. But by midnight she could no longer tolerate the unknown, the fear and the thought that something was obviously wrong, so she called and received the obligatory response. "We'll be there in the morning. Please try to remain calm. She probably is at a friend's or is incommunicado."

Samantha Clark's roommate arrived in the dorm at 9:05am the following morning to move in and prepare for the new semester. Entering the room, she called out, "Sam are you there?" When the door was fully open, the site she witnessed was gruesome and sickening. Lying in a pool of blood was Samantha's naked body on a bed of blood-spattered sheets. Her beautiful blonde hair was drenched with her blood. The bed was completely red and the sheets dripping a magenta red. Her throat was slashed. A cross was carved over her left breast at approximately the level of the heart. Shocked and horrified, the roommate shrieked and shook uncontrollably. Whoever was already checked in at the dorm came running at the sound of the screams to behold this grisly and horrifying discovery.

"Someone, please call the police and an ambulance, hurry," came a cry out of the crowd of few witnesses present. One of the seniors present presented a calming influence and tried to steady everyone assembled. The Southwest Community Station of the LAPD officers arrived a short time later led by Detective John Marin as did an ambulance. But there was obviously little anyone could do medically. Marin called the medical examiner, the crime scene investigator and the forensic pathologist to inspect the dorm room for clues and to secure the scene and confirm that it was free of contamination. At approximately the identical time, the Malibu Sheriff's office had sent Sergeant Mustaf Ali to the Clark home to investigate the missing person report that they had filed. Approximately forty minutes into this interview a detective from the SW Division of the LAPD arrived. When he knocked on the door, he was greeted by a youngish appearing middle aged woman.

"Mrs. Clark, please. I'm Detective Molina from the LAPD."

"I'm Joyce Clark! How can I help you?"

"I see there is another police office already here?"

"Yes. My daughter has been missing since yesterday. She never came home last night."

"May I come in, please?"

"Oh, yes, I'm sorry please, come in."

"I'm sorry. I have some dreadful news for you."

By this time Mr. Edward Clark had joined his wife, Detective Molina and Detective Ali in the conversation in the foyer of the well-appointed modern home. The worried and anxious look on her and her husband's face told him not to hesitate, "I'm so sorry. Your daughter was found in her dorm room this morning. She's dead."

"Dead? Dead? How? What? No. No," Joyce Clark exclaimed as she fell back with her husband grabbing her to hug and comfort her. She burst out screaming and crying as Edward Clark just stared at the detective while trying to comprehend those words. "Sam. Dead?"

"Yes. I am deeply sorry. She was killed in her room and left there. Her roommate found her this morning."

Edward Clark screamed, "What? What are you saying? Who would kill her, a beautiful college freshman without an enemy in the world?"

"We don't know yet, but our investigation has begun. You said she has no enemies Are you absolutely sure? Was she a drug abuser as far as you know? Did she have any boyfriends that she argued or fought with? Were there any recent break-ups with boys, who might want revenge?"

"I don't know what the fuck you're talking about. She was a well-liked, well-adjusted student with lots of friends," replied, Edward Clark with anger at this inquisition.

The detective continued with his interview inquiring about the usual motives and asking about possible suspects although the ghastly nature of this killing made him think that this was not the routine passion killer. There had to be more to it.

When he returned to the station, he discussed his findings with Marin. Marin related his findings. He stated that he learned from her roommate that Samantha was very care-free, sociable and possibly somewhat of a vamp as she had many "boyfriends." He also learned that she was gracious, garrulous and effusive with an unreserved personality. Everyone liked her and enjoyed her company. The roommate could not think of any rivals, enemies or nemeses. The one thing the roommate did mention was the envy many felt for this beautiful, intelligent, rich co-ed with the world at her beckon.

In addition, Marin mentioned that at the end of his perfunctory interviews someone stopped him. He recalled their conversation:

"Please wait. Please."

"Yes, Can I help you?"

"Yes. I know Samantha Clark very well."

"Yes?"

"She was my best friend's girlfriend for a short time last semester."

"OK?"

"That relationship didn't end so well."

"Go on."

"Yes. She cheated on him and he didn't take it well."

"And?"

"And he threatened her."

"What's your friend's name? Is he a student here?"

"His name is Judah Morris, and he goes to Berkeley."

"Berkeley? Is he there now?'

"I don't know, but I think so. I haven't seen him the past week."

"What are you talking about? How is this helpful? If he's at Berkeley how the hell could he be responsible for this?"

"I don't know you're the cop. You figure it put," replied the sarcastic student witness.

"Get out of here."

"What do you think?" Marin asked Molina. "Probably just some crack pot kid trying to put us on a wild goose chase. But I guess, we're obligated to check it out."

Unfortunately, the information required some investigation. They would send one of the sergeants to find this Judah Morris but they both suspected that it would be unrewarding and a dead end. Marin and Molina sat at their desks thinking about this killing. Because of the ritualistic nature of the killing, they put the news on the police blotter to see if there was any evidence of similar killings. Marin also thought this kind of formulaic killing may merit FBI investigation as it pointed to a possible serial killer. He would have to carefully review other reported murders with a similar MO. At his computer while continuing to discuss the case with Molina, Marin checked the California police blotter but found nothing. He then opened a GOOGLE search:

He typed: *Ritualist killing leaving a cross on the chest.*
Three responses appeared on the screen:
NYC killing in East Village.
High School Senior murdered in Beaumont, Mass
Columbia Co-ed found dead in her dorm.

He called out to Molina at this result, "Hey look at this. There is no question that we may very well be dealing with a serial killer. I'm going to call the New York PD and The Beaumont Sheriff's Office for more information," he said while dialing the 6th precinct of the NYPD.

"Hello. This is Detective Marin of the Southern District Station of the LAPD. I'd like to speak to either Detective Saunders or Francis. They are the ones dealing with the killing in the East Village and the one at Columbia, right?" He had learned the detectives involved form the GOOGLE search.

"Yes, That's right, ghastly killings. I'll get Saunders," replied the answering cop.

"Saunders here. Can I help you?"

"Yes. My name is John Marin of the LAPD. We just had a killing at USC with a very similar MO to the ones you're investigating. The victim was a young co-ed, about nineteen, who was murdered in her dorm room. The murderer slashed her throat and probably raped her. In addition, of interest is that he left a cross carved over her chest."

"Shit. In L.A? My God that is the exact MO of our two killings and of another one in Beaumont, Massachusetts."

"Yes. I know. I have a call in for a Capt. Captree."

"Did you call the FBI? This is obviously something the National Center for the Analysis of Violent Crime (NCAVC) and the **FBI's** Critical Incident Response Group (CIRG) needs to learn about and investigate."

"Yes, I did. I called the local bureau and I'm sure they'll contact Quantico. We obviously don't have any further information. But we did get DNA samples as he did rape this poor girl and there was semen available."

"Great. We have semen samples also. Well, thanks for letting us know and please keep us abreast from your end and we'll do the same. We'll contact the NY FBI office also."

Marin sat at his desk as did Saunders at the same time both wondering what was next. They thought it odd that the killer moved to L.A, but also that it shouldn't be that difficult to locate recent L.A. commuters from N.Y. who could fit a psychological profile of a possible serial killer. They were certain that the BAU (Behavioral Analysis Unit) would soon have a profile of the killer, which could very well narrow the search of potential possibilities further. The outstanding issue in their collective minds was preventing the next death. This was most difficult to ascertain since there was no time pattern established for the murders to give them a clue as to when the next killing could possibly take place. Unfortunately, there was no serial timeline to follow. Therefore, all they could do is wait as Captree also imagined. After the call from Marin, Captree remembered his wife's death and the circumstances surrounding it. He thought, *was it possible that her murder was an extension of the latest killings? It was two years ago, and the current murders were in rapid succession, so that was an obvious variance.* The DNA sample that the innocence project sampled would have to be compared to the current samples to prove congruence. He called the project's director and Saunders to suggest they compare the samples of the three murders.

"Hey, Ron, that is a wonderful idea that I didn't even fathom."

"Yeah. Thanks. Will you get the results to me as soon as possible?"

"Sure. By the way, we contacted the FBI, and they should be calling you regarding the Emily O'Connell murder and the facts surrounding it."

The FBI agent in Los Angeles was a dapper, medium height gentleman with piercing eyes, dirty blonde hair and an arrogant manner. He was pretentious and supercilious. Anything anyone volunteered he had already thought of and had an argument for or against it. He mentioned the BAU and their profiling excellence.

"No one is denying that. We just need information right now," retorted Marin.

"That's exactly what we'll do. We'll take it from here."

"Huh? Don't you think that our local station can be helpful to you?"

"Not sure," the pompous agent said laughingly. "This is a national issue as three states are involved and thus outside of your jurisdiction."

"I categorically disagree. As you well know the local police forces were very helpful with the Golden State Killer," Martin empathically replied.

"He fucking confessed. You guys didn't catch him."

"The truth is he was hunted by the Irvine and Santa Barbara County law enforcement agents, so we did have a hand in it. But that is beside the point. This poor girl was killed in L.A., and I think we can be helpful."

"Suit yourself, but BAU will be contacting you soon as they will N.Y. and Beaumont, Mass. Now what have we got?" the agent said with aplomb. The agent proceeded to go the Southern Division of the LAPD. His attitude was no better in person and both Marin and Molina looked at him and shrugged while answering his questions perfunctorily. At the same time the FBI agent presented an entirely different attitude at the 6th precinct and at the Beaumont Sheriff's office. The agent in N.Y especially concentrated on the DNA samples anxiously awaiting the information it could provide. Over the next week, there was no further information gleaned from the autopsy of Samantha Clark. The inquiry at Berkeley was able to confirm that Jonah Morris was registered and had arrived on campus a week prior to Samantha's death, and he claimed he had no contact with her for the past month to six weeks in spite of what the "eye" witness said. Molina and Marin were not discouraged since they had felt this was a blind lead anyway.

To no one's amazement, the DNA samples collected at the Samantha Clark crime scene were identical to the DNA procured at the Columbia dorm room killing of Peg Myrtle. And to the amazement of all the DNA found in Veronica Captree's fingernails was identical to the others. It now appeared that this killer was operating for at least two years prior to the series of recent murders and rapes. In addition, he had appeared to alter his MO somewhat. There was no cross on Veronica Captree's body as evidenced on the others, but everything else was identical, the throat slashing, the rapes, the evidence of semen left and the intense nature of the killing in a formulaic manner. Saunders deduced that this was the profile of a serial killer, probably in his twenties given the previous deaths, probably abused, possibly hating his parents, especially his mother with a religious perversion that might have been only recently revealed. She thought that "cross" signature represented recent religious distortion. Although, the profile was of interest to the parties of the investigation, it hardly t helped to locate him or aid in the assessment of his movements, but Saunders did think that he was possibly a student maybe at Columbia, who transferred to USC recently.

In Beaumont, Sgt. Martin, while combing the Amtrak records of the train of the killing of that poor girl, Jen, did discover an interesting fact. The train from Beaumont approximately on that Thanksgiving weekend had entered Boston at North Station nearly the exact time that the Amtrak to N.Y. left North Station. Maybe a Beaumont commuter was involved in that murder. This could evidently tie in with the original Beaumont killing. It was a long shot but worth the effort of probing further. Sgt. Martin thought it too coincidental that there was a killing on that train with the same MO. He would check the ticket agents and the riders. Maybe, just maybe there was a clue there. Maybe the killer rode form Beaumont to Boston and on to N.Y and killed that unfortunate girl on the way down.

Chapter 14

Sitting at the front desk of Doheny Memorial Library reading a paper on the methods of Sorkin, the famous screenwriter, I couldn't help but perceive a presence hovering over me. I looked up and there was an attractive thirty-something woman with flaming auburn hair, feline eyes of emerald. She was wearing a loose-fitting tank top with tight L'Agence jeans and a Hermes messenger bag with the black strap across her shoulder accentuating her breasts. She was tall and lithe with well-developed muscular arms. She tapped the desk as I pretended not to notice her or her presence or the tap.

"Excuse me!"

Again, while I feigned disinterest, she repeated only this time with more authority, "Excuse me!"

"Uh. I'm sorry. Can I help you?"

"Hmm. What the hell does it take to get your attention? Are you oblivious to the world?"

"Uh. No", I said I was sorry. "What is it I can do for you?"

"Maybe you can help me. My name is Colleen Moore. I work at the sex crime desk for the Los Angeles Times."

"Yes. That doesn't really help me. I'm not really a sex offender or anything like that."

She laughed and said, "No. Of course you're not. I was looking into the murder here at USC. A Samantha Clark was murdered and raped in her dorm room recently."

"Why are you asking me about that? I don't know anything about any murder or rape. I did hear about it in the usual campus pipeline and the news, but why would you come to the library?"

"I was just digging to see what the student body thought about it and the general campus reaction. Can we talk? I'd like to discuss your reaction. I'm going to interview some of the students at the library also. I was hoping to get some insight into the human reaction to a grotesque murder on the campus."

"That seems perverted to me. Sorry, I'm busy and really can't spend any more time with you. Is there anything else I can help you with?"

"What's with the attitude? Sure, Busy, eh? Well, you go back to your book. Thanks!"

As she walked up toward the second floor (probably to interview more unsuspecting students), I felt chagrined. A sense of dread came over me and for the first time since I began this journey, I realized that I would be caught at some point. I obviously wasn't concerned about this intrusive, annoying reporter but the idea of investigating my actions caused me trepidation and unease. Shit, I thought it is inevitable that I will be apprehended, but I have to continue. I can't stop myself. Then a strange sensation came over me. This reporter is nothing but a bitch. What do I do about fucking bitches? I asked myself rhetorically. I slash their fucking throats and enjoy every moment of it. So, I decided to run after her.

"Wait," I yelled. "Hey. I apologize. Wait a moment. Please give me a second chance. Yes, we can talk."

She turned at the top of the stairs and smiled. I returned her smile and ran up the flight two stairs at a time. When I reached her, I smiled again, placed my hand on her shoulder and said, "What do you want to know? We can talk when I finish work in about an hour, can you hang around till then and I'll gladly answer your questions as best I can."

"Sure. That's kind of you."

"No problem. But I don't really know what I can offer a reporter about rape or murder."

"That's okay. I'm only trying to get an appreciation of what students are thinking about with a serial killer on the loose."

"Serial killer?" I asked quizzically and for the first time realizing what exactly I was and what the police, FBI and detectives would be searching for.

"Yes. This USC killing was one of many with very similar characteristics." Moore told me emphatically.

"Really? One of many?" I asked simulating surprise.

"Yes, that's right. There have been at least four if not more. He is being called the **CROSS KILLER** in the media.

I thought, *the Cross Killer, Holy shit they even have a name already*. I better stop this conversation right now as my facial expressions might divulge what I didn't want to reveal. "Wow. Very interesting. Come back downstairs in an hour and we'll talk more," I said realizing the danger and understanding the need to not divulge my true thoughts or feelings.

Colleen Moore approached the Southwest Community Division station of LAPD with the intent to interview Detectives Marin and Molina. She was armed with the webpage from the truecrime. com website with the knowledge that the USC murder of Samantha Clark was hardly an isolated incidence. The MO detailed in the report that she read was nearly identical to a number of other murders in Massachusetts and New York. She was sure that the detectives knew of these. She was also sure that the FBI would get involved if not already investigating. But she needed to inquire how far along the investigation had proceeded; She wanted to know the list of possible suspects if any. And for her story to be authentic she desperately needed the information on leads, DNA evidence, murder weapon, autopsy results, etc. She obviously knew they would be loath to reveal anything of import, but her meddling would be invaluable to the paper and her readers. She aspired to be first to break the story of a nationwide manhunt for a serial rapist/killer that was sure to go viral and become a huge deal. Her byline would be prominent and widely quoted. She had little regard for the consequences of her actions or the position of the LAPD. They had a job to do and so did she. Many had called her ruthless, devious and unscrupulous. But did not journalism always elicit similar criticism. She cared little for the pronouncements of the police or their reaction. She waked briskly to the station excited and captivated by the possibilities. She knew that breaking this huge story would garner her many possibilities of advancement and that was paramount above all else. She entered the station and asked the desk sergeant for Molina and Marin. He picked up his intercom and announced, "Detective Molina, please call the front desk." And the called out, "Detective Marin, please call the front desk." After a few moments, the desk phone rang and the sergeant said, "Hey, Ray there's an attractive chick here to see you." Moore was infuriated at the sexism and misogyny but accepted it as the norm for the LAPD. "My name is Colleen Moore and I'm a reporter for LA Times, please!"

"Oh yeah, I'm sorry. She's a reporter for the LA Times."

"I got nothing to say to her," came the reply, load enough for her to hear.

"Tell him that I know a lot about the case involving Samantha Clark and will stay here all night if I have to in order to get some information. Let him know that tomorrow's paper will detail a serial killer in Los Angeles and will obviously frighten the shit out of this community especially if I only publish what I know, which is rudimentary and could cause more alarm."

"Shit, just what the fuck I need. Okay, okay. Send her back," came the muffled voice on the other end. The desk sergeant led her to the Homicide Division and knocked on the door.

"Come in", said a voice in the room.

The medium height, mustachioed man wearing a blue suit, blue shirt and red tie, sitting behind a cluttered desk in large room with three other desks, displayed quite an attitude with his body language.

"What do you want?' he asked.

"I have a few questions about the Samantha Clark murder," Moore said thinking that this is exactly what she expected from this well-known misogynist detective.

As Colleen Moore looked around the Homicide Division, she could feel the detective's anger and mistrust.

"Yes? Moore you said, right?" asked the detective, who was a fairly good-looking generation Xer.

"Hello, Detective Molina. Yes, I'm Colleen Moore of the LA Times."

"Oh yeah, I read your column occasionally. It's hardly a murder or crime related column, but rather it encompasses a more psychological bent with a human-interest twist."

"Yes. That's right. I'm writing an article on the psychology of the sexual predator," said Moore.

"So, you lied to weasel your way in here. I don't deal in psychology and couldn't help you at all in that department."

"I know that. I'll be going to USC to interview students for that. But this case intrigues and frightens me and I thought I would check out some details about it since our readers are probably very interested. Serial killer stories always grab the public's interest."

"Details? You expect me to give you details about a cold case. You really don't know shit about homicide investigation. Do you?"

"Whatever information you can give me would be really helpful and appreciated."

"Well, here it is! We know shit at the present time and that's what you'll know after this interview."

"Do you have DNA?'

"We have what we have," Molina replied.

"What about a murder weapon? Any luck finding it yet?" asked Moore.

"Hmm," said Molina.

"Is the FBI involved?"

"Yes."

"Well, that's something. Who is the agent? Never mind I can find that out on my own. Is there anything else that you would like to add to this scintillating conversation?"

"I told you. You get nada."

"Okay, Detective Molina, I'll let you return to paperwork there. Thank you"

She left the station nonplussed at his surliness and attitude, but hardly surprised. She drove the six miles back to the LA Times headquarters thinking of the story she would write tonight.

Colleen Moore walked down to the front desk of the library and sitting there waiting for her was that insolent student, she had spoken to previously, who suggested she return in an hour. He was now very cooperative.

"Hey, I'm back maybe a little early but close to the hour," she stated.

"Ah, yes, the reporter is back. What can I do for you? What do you want to know and how can I possibly help?" I asked.

"I have a few questions. Would you like to go somewhere to chat?" Moore replied.

"Sure. I just have a few things to finish up here and I'll join you. Where shall I meet you?" I asked expectantly but with some trepidation.

"Do you know El Huevo's?"

"I'm pretty new here, but I'll find it. Meet you there in half hour or so."

On the way to the restaurant, Ms. Collen Moore imagined the article she was about to write. It was obviously much different than her usual column but tantalizing nonetheless:

The Cross Killer Terrorizes L.A

After multiple deaths in New York and Massachusetts deemed at the hand of a serial killer, Los Angeles now has its first victim. A nineteen-year-old USC co-ed was found murdered in her dorm room. Although kept secret by the LAPD, the MO of this killing was very similar to the cases in New York and Beaumont, Massachusetts. The signature of the killer is a cross carved on the left chest wall over the heart of the victims. The LAPD would not say anything about the investigation although it appears that adequate DNA samples have been procured. There are no suspects and there is no murder weapon found thus far. The cases identified, thus far, are in their late teens to early twenties. There was another co-ed from Columbia University found in her dorm room. In addition, a high school senior from Beaumont, Mass was found in an isolated area in an arboretum. A mid-twenty aged woman was found on the Northeast Amtrak line on its way to the Newark Airport stop. Another twenty-something woman was found in the East Village. That victim is said to be a prostitute. Every victim's throat was slashed. The victims were all raped, some possibly posthumously. The ritualistic identifier for all the killings is a cross carved on the left chest over the heart of the victims. The police recommend that all young women be aware of these events and take extreme precautions with strangers. The LAPD is working with the NYPD, the Beaumont sheriff's office and the FBI to profile this killer and identify psychological characteristics that would aid in identifying this psychopath. The LAPD requests that all information volunteered be discreetly sent or called to the following number: 661-555-1221.

Her original ideas were well thought out and well written although melodramatic, but she felt that the story needed that. Not only is there a killer on the loose but a maniacal one at that. She knew the article would create panic but then again it would also create an identity for her and for her reporting. She was excited and enthusiastic about its potential effect on her career. That could not be denied. Thus, she would continue to pursue it and to hell with the cops and their investigation. Why should she give a shit, if there is suddenly panic and fear in Los Angeles, generally and the USC campus specifically and that the cops are angered by her reporting. Los Angeles needs to know this story.

She entered El Huevo's, greeted the hostess and sat at the designated table and waited for the young man. As she did, she again rehashed the article in her mind, took out her laptop and began typing her story. She wanted to get it out for the morning edition if possible. There had been some reporting of the campus murder but only as a page ten article and very superficially reported. Her article would break open the case for the public. In addition, the psychological profile of the students would add a dramatic sense to the entire picture of this developing ominous story.

While she was intently typing, adding and deleting phrases, I walked into the restaurant, scanned the room found that electrifying auburn hair and the bright yellow tank top, now without the strap draping over her breasts and walked over.

"Hey."

"Hey. Thanks for coming."

"I said I would."

"Yes, yes you did. Well thanks anyway," Collen Moore said agreeably.

"So, what can I help you with?" I asked expectantly.

"As I told you a Samantha Clark was murdered in her dorm at USC."

"Yes. I know you said that. What can I help you with? Why did you want to speak to me? Is there really anything I can offer you regarding that murder?"

"Well. This appears to be the act of a serial killer. There have been several other similar killings on the East Coast."

"And?"

"I've spoken to the LAPD and am about to publish a headline article for the LA Times. In order to add human interest, I have been interviewing students to get an appreciation for their thoughts, fears and feelings about the USC campus under these conditions. I wanted your perspective since you have such visible access to the student body in your duties at the library."

"Why would you think that there will be others at USC?"

"I don't, but I just thought the reaction of the students would interest my readers. I also intend to get reactions from the general public in the USC environs."

"Well. I'm not a young woman, who is about to be raped so I'm not sure I'm the best person to talk to."

"I agree. But you can offer a male perspective of what one must be thinking and feeling in order to commit such heinous crimes. In addition, I was wondering whether you've heard any talk or gossip about what the students are feeling."

"Have you gotten a female perspective, yet?"

"Of course."

"May I ask what you learned?" I asked trying to gauge her knowledge and understanding of the mind of the killer.

Colleen Moore responded hesitantly as she did not want to influence my answer, "There is general consternation among the students that I've spoken to. Women seem to feel a foreboding and therefore, have congregated more, refused to be alone for prolonged periods of time and tend more diligently to their safety, carefully paying attention to their associations. But what do you think?"

I answered knowing full well that what I was about to say could easily be misconstrued and lead to my misfortune. Thinking about it, I had no rationale for my honesty and openness only my confidence, anxiety, anger and maybe even my narcissism: "Well to be entirely frank, I have read multiple psychological profiles of serial killers. The fear factor you're finding out from your interviews is exactly what most serial killers wish to uncover. This charges their acts and enables and empowers them. The anger at their victims seems to stem from deep seated distrust and hatred for authorities-possibly parents, teaches, employers, etc. This will lead to transference of that hatred into acts of violence. This is especially true for heinous crimes against women."

"Shit. That sounds like you've been studying this behavior for a long time and at your age. Are you interested in psychology or criminology?

"No. Not at all. I'm a writer."

"Well, thank you so much for talking to me. That is most enlightening. May I quote you on your thoughts?" she asked.

"Absolutely not. Don't you ever mention my name or any possible identifiers! What I have told you has to be strictly anonymous. Understand?" I said vehemently and emphatically.

"No problem. I understand and fully will comply with your wishes," she replied.

"I would suggest if you intend to investigate or write about a serial killer you research it more." I said confidently and assuredly in spite of our difference in age and experience.

She looked at me in amazement at my arrogance, but my sole intent was to impress her and try to establish a further relationship. "Hey, I'm only teasing. I've read your stuff and you seem to be a very effective journalist and I realize this is new territory for you. Maybe, we can get together sometime and discuss this further."

She looked at me astonishingly, "I don't think so. I don't get involved with young arrogant twerps." I laughed and suggested Friday night at 6pm at the library entrance. She stared at me, shook her head and snickered.

"See you then, Colleen."

Martin rushed a long printout of the Amtrak schedule and the ticketed passengers into Crabtree's office. "Ronald. Here is the printout of the ticketed passengers on that Amtrak train which pulled into Newark Airport Station with a dead woman on it. Remember? Look at these names!"

Chapter 15

During an especially intense marathon of studying for mid-terms, I was suddenly disturbed by my phone's loud chime.

My concentration broken, I cursed at the goddam phone.

"Yes! Who the hell is it?"

"Hey, Dicks, relax. What's eating you?"

"Oh Shit! Sorry professor. I was in the middle of an intense study time and the phone broke my concentration," I said apologetically.

"No worries, Dicks. I just heard from my contact at Netflix. They're very anxious to meet you to discuss your script.

"Discuss my script? You have got to be kidding me. I'm barely nineteen and the content coordinator at Netflix wants to discuss my script. Holy shit! What do I do next professor?"

"You go to Netflix headquarters," Professor Bergman said pragmatically.

"I'll have to get someone to help me. You're not going to be in Los Angeles any time soon, are you?"

Bergman laughed and said, "Not a chance. I hate that city. Ask your parents."

"Oh! Well, I'm not actually speaking to them. But I have an idea. You know a Professor Steinfeld at UCLA, don't you? I met him on my flight out to L.A and mentioned that you were friends and gave me his card after we spoke about you."

"Ah, yes. Monroe is a dear friend of mine. He probably was on that plane after attending a conference in New York that we both attended."

"I guess. He offered to help me after I told him about your critique of my script."

"That's a wonderful idea. He has many contacts in the film and television industry as he probably told you. You would think a college professor lives pretty meagerly in California. But old Monroe owns a home in Beverly Hills. So, I would say he indeed has contacts. Congrats Dicks and keep me abreast of the developments. How is the film school at USC? You knocking them dead? Take care and best of luck. I think you're on your way to quite a career. By the way did you show Monroe the script?"

"No. Not yet. But I intend to as soon as I speak to him."

He gave me the contact information for Eugene Warren, the talent and content coordinator at Netflix and hung up while I sat there in shock and amazement. I was overjoyed at this development and needed to tell someone.

So, feeling that my concentration was already broken, I decided to call Maria and my parents. This was not something that I could keep from them in spite of our differences and the antagonistic way I had left. My mother did contact me a few times and our conversations were cursory and perfunctory, but I have to admit non combative.

Assuredly, I felt the first person to tell would have to be Maria. I would try to convince her to join me at Netflix headquarters and spend some time with me in California afterwards. It was probably an imprudent thought knowing well the intensity of the Columbia curriculum and her dedication to her grades and studies. But I would ask anyway.

I dialed her number and thought about what I would say.

Anxiously I said, "Maria? Hey, it's Evan. I have some wonderful news."

"Evan. It's so good to hear from you. I have to admit I miss you too. How are you doin?"

"I'm great. Yeah, but please listen! I just got off the phone with Bergman. He said that the contact coordinator at Netflix wants to meet me and discuss my script."

"Bullshit!" she exclaimed in disbelief.

"No, No. really. It's true and I think it would be absolutely great if you could join at their headquarters in Los Gatos, California."

"Los who, what?"

"Gatos. It's near San Jose in Silicon Valley."

"When are you going? I'm pretty swamped here."

"I thought so, but we can arrange it for some time during Spring Break."

"I don't know," she replied hesitantly.

"Please think about it, ok? How are you? How are classes? USC is so much easier than Columbia and the lovely Southern California weather is absolutely ideal. My classes are great especially the writing and film classes."

"I'm fine, but as I said swamped just trying to keep up with the Core let alone the other courses, but the campus is great, and I have made a bunch of new friends."

"No boyfriends, I hope," I said sheepishly.

"Oh no," she said laughingly, "Not a chance."

"Hey, listen Mare, I have to tell my parents about the Netflix gig. I'll call you back after I speak to them, ok?"

"You're calling your mom? That's great. I hope this leads to a reconciliation, don't you? Anyway, thanks for calling me first and take care. I love you."

"What did you just say?" I asked.

"I love you."

"Maria. I miss you and love you too. I think."

"Hmm!" she said.

"Bye mi amor. I'll speak to you soon," I said hanging up.

As I dialed my home, my anxiety rose to an immeasurable level. My mom answered and I spoke. "Hi, mom. Its Evan."

"Evan. My Evan."

"Yes, Mom. Evan Dicks."

"It's so good to hear your voice. How are you? Are you eating and sleeping enough? Do you have enough money?"

"Mom. One question at a time. I'm doing great. I am eating and sleeping, and I have a job at the library which helps with incidentals. How are dad and Jimmy?"

"We're all good and we miss you terribly."

"Thanks, Mom. I have some wonderful news. Netflix invited me to discuss my script for possible production."

I heard a thud as if she dropped the phone and then heard her yell, "Tom, Tom! It's Evan. He was invited to meet with Netflix to discuss his script for possible production. Here please speak to him," she said while giving the phone to my dad.

"Hello Evan. Is that true? That is fantastic news. Maybe I did misjudge you and your talent. When is this coming about?"

"I haven't set it up yet. Dr. Bergman from Columbia introduced me to a guy named Warren, who is the coordinator for content acquisition at Netflix. I'm going to call him to set up the meeting after finals this semester. As I told you, he thought my script was special and that it might make a fine film or TV series."

"Uh Huh," he said cynically returning to his true nature.

"Don't sound so enthusiastic, dad."

"Do you want me to feign excitement when I think my son is wasting his time with this shit rather than pursuing a real career? Sorry, son. No can do, even though you might have some talent. I think this is a dead end with little reward."

"Thanks, dad, for those wonderful words of encouragement. I'll be seeing you."

"Good luck to you, Evan."

I then heard my mom screaming, "Wait. I want to say goodbye and wish him well."

Unfortunately, her screams and pleas were to no avail. I heard the phone click and go dead.

Colleen Moore sat on her suede couch with a glass of chardonnay completing the draft of her piece on the Cross Killer. She finished the final sentence; proofread it again, copied it onto the e-mail account of the Metro editor of the LA Times with a note:

Enclosed is the article on the Cross Killer, please note the similarities of the USC murder with several others from the East Coast. I also included some interviews of a few USC students. Please pay special attention to the male freshman, who works at Doheny Library. I think, given the gravity of the killing and the serial nature of the MO, this merits front page. Hope you agree.

My Best, Col.

She sat back bemused by her investigative excellence and pressed send on her Dell Pro. While undressing, she started thinking about the strange, curious, reticent kid, who gave a professorial dissertation on the psychology of a serial killer. She thought it perplexing and enigmatic that this nineteen-year-old had the foresight and understanding of a mature, seasoned research psychologist and serial killer profiler. She considered that maybe there was more to this intriguing character than met the eye. Maybe she ought to not dismiss him so readily. Maybe he understood more about these crimes than was apparent with only one singular superficial discussion. As she brushed her teeth in her modern completely gray marble bathroom with American Standard fixtures, she decided to meet him again. She would accept his offer and meet him again with the condition being further discussion of his knowledge. She asked herself what his intentions could be. She couldn't answer that question but had to proceed and discover the answer. She understood that what she was doing was quite bizarre, but she rationalized it as being part of her job and research. She laughed and said, *"Sure, Col. He is just an interviewee and nothing more. Justification accepted."* Did she really think that she was interested in fucking him? She was intrigued by the thought, but she laughed shook her head, and dismissed that ridiculous scenario.

I called Steinfeld and he was very happy to hear of my good fortune and felt we should be to discuss the logistics of meeting Netflix and the script. He also requested a copy of the manuscript to review.

"Hi, Professor Steinfeld. This is Evan Dicks. I just hung up with Professor Bergman, who suggested I speak to you further after you graciously offered to help me navigate a possible Netflix production of my screenplay."

"Oh, yes. I remember. You're the fine lad on the transcontinental flight to LAX."

"Yes. Well anyway, Professor Bergman said that Eugene Warren, the Talent and Content Coordinator at Netflix wanted to meet me to discuss possible production of my screenplay. Dr. Bergman suggested I give you a call given your contacts and obvious understanding of the film and television industry."

"Thank you. I'd be glad to help out. When is your meeting scheduled for?"

"I have yet to schedule it, but I was thinking maybe Spring Break so it won't interfere with my classes and as an ulterior motive, I was hoping my girlfriend could join me for a mini vacation of sorts. I haven't seen her since December. She goes to Columbia and lives in New York."

"Great. That gives us some time. First, I'd like to read the treatment and critique. Even though

I implicitly trust Bergman, I want a personal perspective of your work. You understand that I'm helping you because of my friendship with Bergman but should something come of this we can discuss some sort of compensation."

"Absolutely! I would expect to reimburse for your time and effort as I would everyone who helped me."

"Let's you and I meet, and you can give me a copy of the screenplay and discuss it at a future date."

"No need. I could email or fax it to you, so we don't waste too much time."

"Great."

He then gave me his email address and we set up an appointment in his office at UCLA.

Sitting at the research desk at Doheny and doing a paper on the films of Goddard, I felt a tap on my shoulder. I looked up and standing there was that beautiful LA Times reporter I had met one week earlier.

"I decided to accept your invitation," she said awkwardly.

"Hmm. Well. That is a surprise. I wasn't expecting that at all," I said.

"Yeah. I guess? I was just fascinated by your comments on the Cross Killer and wanted to examine them further."

"Great. Let me finish up here and we can leave. Where did you want to go?"

"I thought we could grab a pizza and go back to my apartment." she said pragmatically.

"I was astonished at this presumptuousness, especially given our age difference, but I was surely not going to contend the point."

"I can drive if it's ok with you," she remarked.

"Sure! Who am I to argue with an LA Times reporter of renown?"

"Hardly," she responded more assuredly.

We left the library headed for the visitor parking lot and at the far end, she pointed out a gray Honda Civic.

"I hope you don't mind my frugal wheels. They don't exactly pay us extraordinary wages at the newspaper."

"Hey. I'm not one to protest. Me, only a lowly college freshman? No way."

After picking up a margherita pizza, we drove the fifteen miles to Sunset Blvd, and she turned onto Crescent to a side street to a modest Town House. We entered her apartment, and it was surprisingly well-furnished in expensive tastes with a suede couch and a well-appointed kitchen with a small eating space. She dropped the pizza carton on the kitchen table and asked if I would like a beer.

"Sure" I replied not surprised at the offer although I was under aged. I sat down at the table. She brought out some porcelain dishes and flat ware and served the pizza with a beer for herself and one for me.

This whole experience seemed surreal to me. I couldn't understand what her motivation was or what I was doing there, but I accepted that she found me interesting and wanted to converse further and maybe pick my brain after I so impressed her initially. My naiveté and taciturn personality did not seem to bother her, but my own thought did confuse me. Finishing my pizza, a continuing thought prevailed:

I was not an introverted, taciturn, reticent, and awkward kid any longer. I was "killer", literally and figuratively. Here was this modern, good looking, sophisticated woman nearly twice my age and yet happily willingly to be with me. I even think she wants to fuck me. Otherwise, what's with the beer and her apartment? My confidence continued to grow.

"Hey, are you there?" she asked taping me on the shoulder.

"Huh? Oh yes, sorry."

"I asked you about your life and family."

"Ah. I just had these strange thoughts. Yes. My life and family."

"You want to share your strange thoughts?" she asked.

"No not really. They're private crazy thoughts. Anyway, I grew up in Beaumont, Mass and went to school at Beaumont High. I graduated as the salutatorian and went to Columbia for the first semester last year. I'm interested in becoming an author, and I wrote a screenplay for my level two creative writing class and my professor loved it and sent it to a friend of his at Netflix. They want to meet me to discuss the possibility of producing it. Thus, subsequently, I transferred to the USC film school and here I am."

"What became of the screenplay?"

"Well," I replied sheepishly, "they invited me to pitch the idea to Eugene Warren, the talent and content coordinator."

"Holy shit! You're only fucking what eighteen or nineteen. That's fucking amazing. You're already fucking further along than me, who has been writing for the LA times for eight years."

I must have been blushing and cowering as she came over and petted and kissed my cheek, I responded with a passionate kiss on her lips slipping my tongue into her mouth. She was immediately taken aback and recoiled as her first reaction but after a moment's hesitation, she grabbed my hand and led me into her bedroom. Now it was I who was nonplussed, and I eagerly followed. When we got to the bedroom, she pushed me unto the bed and took off my worn Columbia tea shirt. She removed her blouse and revealed two beautiful loose breasts, perfectly champagne glass shaped with protruding nipples. She unbuttoned my jeans and straddled me. The act was natural and not at all unexpected. She finished with a loud pronounced, "God!" and fell off of me. When I regained my composure, I reached for my jeans to find my switchblade. While she lay there with her eyes closed in post coital bliss, I slashed her throat. Blood began spurting everywhere and I heard a loud gasp emanating from her mouth. Her eyes widened with the shock and fear evident. I then entered her again. I felt the surge in my loins begin and that release again. I thought about carving the cross on her chest as she took her last breath. Debating this, a bizarre and surprising thought entered my mind:

Did I just kill this woman for religious reasons because she was immoral in seducing a teenager? Not at all, I killed her because I enjoy it. I get tremendous pleasure from the power over women and that picture of their anguish, fear and shock.

Therefore, having decided that, I didn't leave my ritualistic cross all the while wondering how this might affect the investigation. Would the LAPD and possibly FBI think this was an isolated incident or part of the pattern now recognized as the Cross Killer? I didn't really care. I left her apartment hurriedly but contented.

Chapter 16

Spring break couldn't come fast enough. I had arranged my Netflix meeting for the week after Easter Sunday. Maria accepted my invitation and plane tickets to join me on this extraordinary adventure of my young life. With the help of Steinfeld, I was able to secure the rights of "Deadly Motivations" from the author for a stake in the royalties. The author, J. Paul Bradley was an interesting fellow. He lived in New York and was a Hematology/Oncology fellow at Memorial Sloan-Kettering Cancer Center. He had started the book between his first and second year of internal medicine residency at Weill-Cornell Medical center and completed it at the end of his third year. It was a bit of surprise that he the time to write a novel while a medical resident, but he had said there were extenuating health issues that allowed the time, He never expected that it would sell. He self-published the manuscript and it died online with middling sales. So, hearing from me, he was naturally shocked and pleasantly surprised and obviously receptive to Steinfeld's and my proposal. His time commitment to the fellowship would not allow him to join me for my pitch to Netflix but I promised I would keep him well apprised of the outcome. I promised Bradley that if Netflix accepted my proposition, I would solicit his aid in completing the screenplay for production if he wished in order to get a writing credit. Steinfeld felt this was a proper direction for a first-time screenwriter and that this gesture would garner good will with Bradley and the industry. The entire contract with Bradley for the rights was based on contingency without upfront money, which I obviously didn't have, or any guarantees. We completed the transaction by phone, Zoom and Fax, the modern technology way. I drove to the airport in a Zipcar. (I have to mention at this juncture that the job at the library was really helpful for my finances. By this time, my parents had pretty much stopped sending me any support). Waiting at the baggage claim, I spotted her, that long haired, tan skinned beauty, who I had grown so fond of. As she searched for her bag, I ran up to her, hugged her and kissed her.

"Maria! Maria. It's been so goddam long. I've missed you so much."

"Hey, Ev. Me too. It's so wonderful to see you. I am so excited for you. I can't believe that Netflix is really interested in your manuscript."

"Yeah. I'm very excited, too. But fuck that. We have so much to catch up on. How are you? How is school? How's your family?"

"Hey. One sec. Let me get my bag and then we'll go to your place, and we can catch up on the way."

"Yeah, so sorry. I just got carried away seeing you again. Not cool, eh?"

"Don't be so puerile. Of course, your enthusiasm is cool."

"What an impressive vocabulary. Columbia must be rubbing off on you."

"Come on. Stop. I'm the same Queens girl that I've always been."

"Yeah, and I'm the same naïve shit that you first met."

"Are you saying you're not? What are you saying? You've become a sophisticated shit instead?"

"Hardly," I replied laughingly.

We walked to the short-term parking lot at LAX, entered the gray Prius and drove onto RT. 105. Our trip was animated with conversation. We reviewed the past three and half months in exceeding detail. We discussed her courses, the enjoyable ones and the "painful" ones. We discussed her recent dates, which she admitted to grudgingly. I discussed my film history course, introductory screenwriting course (which she stated I hardly needed given that I was about to pitch a treatment to Netflix and probably sign a huge deal). When she asked about my love life, dates and friends, I hesitatingly mentioned Samantha Clark but only in passing as an acquaintance with one prior date. I never mentioned her death or murder. When she mentioned the story she heard about a possible serial killer terrorizing the USC campus, I feigned ignorance and mentioned that I had heard something about the murders but was not entirely clear on the details. Obviously, she didn't recognize the name Samantha Clark as the victim's identity had yet to be released. She looked at me quizzically and asked how I could be so uninformed and seemingly unconcerned. I told her I was concerned and that there was a buzz around the campus, but I quickly changed the subject to the killings back on the Columbia campus inquiring about news of those. She told me that as yet they were still unsolved and there was continuing terror on the campus, but that she had little contact with since she continued to live at home. We dined at a diner near my dorm and retired to my room for the evening. We made love that night passionately with an urgency that I had never experienced previously with her. She, too, sensed a difference and commented that our relationship was surely taking a turn, which she claimed gratified her. Her comments and her intensity surprised and pleased me. My confidence continued to grow.

"Good night sweet, Maria. Te amo."

"Good night, Evan. I love you too."

As her words slowly evaporated into the silence, I closed my eyes and gradually drifted into a trancelike state.

"Evan, It's time for bed. Please get ready and I'll meet you in the bathroom for your bath."

"Okay, Mom."

I entered the bathroom; the bath was full and filled with warm but not scalding water three-quarters the way up. Mom was standing in a bathrobe waiting for me. "Come in, Evan. Take off you robe and go into the bath." She took off her robe and climbed into the bathtub herself, naked. I entered beside her. She grabbed my hand and slowly moved it over her abdomen and up to her chest and breasts, lingering over the nipple of her left breast. She then massaged my face, chest, abdomen and penis with her other hand.

"Doesn't that feel good, Evan?"

"Yes, mom," I acknowledged in my confused and bewildered state. She had given me a bath many times previously and had even massaged my back, abdomen and chest, but this was the first time she had ever been in the bath with me and the first time she stroked my penis.

She then slid my hand down to her vagina and into its cavity. She moved my hand rapidly over the area above the opening. After a few moments, I felt her shudder and heard her say," Oh my, Oh my."

All I could do is just sit there perplexed at what was happening but feeling very unnerved and alarmed, startled and terrified.

"She appreciated my anxiety and proclaimed, "That's all right, Evan, everything is fine. Don't be alarmed or frightened. Mommy loves you very much."

"Yes, mommy, I know. You'll always protect me from daddy's beating, right?"

"Yes, Evan. I'll always be here for you."

I awoke in a cold sweat. It had been many years since I had thought about that incident and yet it explicated so much. I bounced up from the bed and ran to the bathroom, ran some cold water and washed my face vigorously. Luckily, I didn't wake Maria not having a plausible explanation. I walked back to the bed, reclined and spent the rest of the night in a fitful state. I tossed and turned the next four hours and finally gave up, showered, dressed in a blue blazer, white Polo oxford, open at the collar and cordovan tasseled loafers. I sat at my laptop rehearsing my pitch to Netflix awaiting Maria's rise. She awoke at 7am, dressed in a blue jumper to match my blazer (she said) with a white top and penny loafers. I wondered whether we looked the hip couple or just two young inexperienced, naïve teenagers who were going to get their asses handed to them by the sophisticated adults in the room. I didn't think it mattered since I had an adult with us for support and I was the one with the script.

When Maria and I arrived at the Beverly Hills Hotel, we inquired the whereabouts of the

Champagne Room, where our meeting with Eugene Warren was to take place. Monroe Steinfeld was already seated at the oval table. Each place was set with a Beverly Hills Hotel engraved pad, pencil, glasses with ice for the pitcher of water placed in the center. There was also a small cup of flavored mints.

Seinfeld greeted me with a warm, salutation, "Evan Dicks! It is so good to see you again. I must tell you; I totally agree with Bergman. Your treatment was extraordinary. This suspenseful story would make an excellent film or even an original series. Do you think you can extend the plot further? Obviously, the author meant for it to be continued with a sequel, which I presume he has yet to write. At the ending when the agent becomes airborne, the implications are the development of a worldwide pandemic. This surely can lead to an extended storyline and ripe for a possible original series. What do you think?"

"Yes, that's right. When I spoke to him after we signed the contract for the rights, I did mention this to him and suggested we could work on it together."

"Are you sure you want to share the screenwriting credits with someone else?" he asked.

"Who am I? I am just so excited to be in this position that I'll accept anything that makes sense. That's why I am so pleased that you're here helping me."

"Give yourself some credit. This is a great treatment of an interesting story. I've never read the novel, but your screenplay is extremely literate, well written and will be easily translated into an excellent film or series."

"Thank you so much for the vote of confidence," I exclaimed.

"Evan, I am so proud of you. This is so exciting." Maria was just finishing her compliment when an impressively tall, tanned, trim man strolled in.

"I'm Eugene Warren with Netflix," the tall man said emphatically.

"Good morning. I'm Evan Dicks. I believe you know Monroe Steinfeld, and this is my girlfriend form New York, Maria Lopez," I stated as he sat at the head of the table, took out a laptop, logged in and then looked up at me.

He was wearing pressed tight designer jeans and pink golf shirt without a label and a gray sweater jacket that was open and loose. His hair was cut short with a small greying pompadour and greying temples. He had a very short, trimmed beard almost imperceptible.

"Hey Dr. Steinfeld. How are you? Are you finally bringing me something worthwhile today? The other stuff you recommended was shit," he said laughing.

"You're a son of a bitch, Warren. Well, I have to tell you this is one of the most exciting scripts I've read in a long time. It has everything, suspense, a love interest, a pandemic, science and mystery. In addition, it is so well written.

"Yeah, yeah, yeah. We'll see. Okay Dicks! What you got?"

I stood up, checked my notes and started my pitch. I knew that Warren had read the script since Bergman had sent him a copy a while ago, but I was presenting as if the story and script were totally unfamiliar to him:

"This script is based on a novel called, "Deadly Motivations" by J. Paul Bradley. We have obtained the rights to the novel and have Bradley's blessing to produce the story and take it any direction that you deem feasible. The protagonist is Daniel Whitacore, a brilliant hematologist/oncologist, who discovers a new therapy for lymphoma and Hodgkin disease based on the immune response to a prion. That is the agent that causes "Mad Cow Disease". He rearranges the agent's DNA so it's non-infectious but retains its immune responsiveness and thus, enhances the body's defenses to the lymphoma. The agent is purloined, forced back into its native state and used by the group that stole the prion, a Bio-terrorist organization, to cause a pandemic. There are multiple players involved in the plot to develop and test the agent, including many who Whitacore trusts such as his fellow and his fellow's girlfriend a Harvard educated PhD, who is well versed in science, but also in human foibles and of course, sex. The story was written open-ended with room for a sequel and continuation, but very easily can reach a dénouement as is."

"To be honest, I have read your script after Bergman sent it to me and found it very producible. I especially liked the open-endedness that you describe. Let me ask you. Did you ask Bradley whether any of this is plausible? He's a physician, right?"

"Yes, he is, and we did discuss that. He suggested that currently the therapy of cancer is undergoing a marked change towards utilization of the immune system as a therapy and away from chemotherapy. This allows the treatment to be nonspecific to the cancer type and also could improve the therapeutic index. So that part is very feasible. Whether a prion or provirus can be manipulated to elicit a specific immune response to lymphoma and be injected into tumors or tumor environments as therapy is conjecture."

"I see, but I don't necessarily think that matters as science fiction can be just as popular as reality and as we've seen science fiction very often becomes science fact," Warren continued.

"I agree. Even if it is totally implausible, how real are zombies? But I believe that for a lay audience the prospect of a pandemic could generate significant anxiety and thus, popularity."

"Good point," said Steinfeld.

There was a moment of silence that elicited an obvious anxious look on my face at which point Warren remarked, "Well. I must tell you that you're an impressive young man; I realize that this story is not yours and the ideas are those of Bradley, but your treatment is superb and has great potential. I have spoken to our production team and our CEO, and I am pleased to tell you that we would like to proceed. I suggest you hire a lawyer and an agent. We'll send you the contracts and I'm hoping we can get started this summer."

Stunned and nearly speechless, I just sat there not having the words to describe my surprise, amazement, astonishment and elation of that pronouncement.

Steinfeld chimed in, "Don't worry Evan, I can help you secure representation."

"No to be disrespectful but I need to call my parents and get their advice," I said reverting to the teenager I really was and hoping to garner parental approval and support.

"Understood," he acknowledged.

"So, if we're good, I'll be in touch in the next few weeks to finalize the contracts, scheduling and logistics of proceeding. Congratulation Mr. Dicks and fine job" Warren checked his gold Patek-Phillipe Calatrava wristwatch, which I discerned by its characteristic face, arose and left the meeting room, "Ciao."

I sat there smiling at Maria only able to mouth "Wow."

"Evan. This is unbelievable. I can't begin to tell you how proud I am of you."

"Thanks, Maria. Let's celebrate. Professor Steinfeld, would you like to join us?"

"No. I'm sorry. I'm swamped. Sone other time though. Make sure to call if you need help with an agent or a lawyer. By the way, good luck to you and you do indeed deserve this. You're a fine writer."

I looked at him leaving, waved a shy good-bye and said, "Thank you so much. I will call my parents and get back to you if I need further assistance. I'll also mention to Bergman what a tremendous help you were. Thanks again."

Professor Monroe Steinfeld left the room as Maria and I sat a while longer in amazement and shock at this development. We then arose and followed him out. We spent the rest of the day exploring Los Angeles. We took a cab to Santa Monica Beach and spent part of the day on the boardwalk. We people watched and enjoyed the warm eighty-degree weather, the cloudless sky and the tacos in a small taqueria on Santa Monica Blvd. and then decided to walk the three miles to Venice. Maria and I were amazed at the contrast. The upscale urban feel of Santa Monica Beach morphed into a circus- like atmosphere: a potpourri of street performers, tattoo parlors, artists peddling their work and marijuana dispensaries. People were walking, jogging, roller skating and just hanging out. I'm not sure I had ever seen anything as unique as this beach. Maria concurred as we laughed, hugged and kissed. We sat on the warm white sand as the sun set over the Pacific Ocean into a magenta hue, lost in our thoughts. I thought about the call I was to make to my parents to tell them that their son had sold a piece of work to be produced on Netflix. I thought about what their reaction would be and their response to my need for a lawyer and agent. Frankly based on my previous experiences, I dreaded the encounter. Maria thought about California, its lifestyle, weather and the possibility of living here. We seemed to fall asleep in the sand for a while.

"I told you to clean this mess in your room, didn't I?"

"Yes, Dad. I'm trying."

"Bullshit. I told you yesterday, the day before and again this morning and you haven't even scratched the fucking surface." He slapped my face and punched me in the arm. I cried out, "Okay, okay. Give me a chance." My thin nine-year-old frame was shaking with fear and pain, but he was unrelenting. He hit my head again and slammed me onto the bed and punched my face at the cheekbone. I screamed, "Please, please stop!!"

"I'll stop when I'm done with you."

"Mom, mom help."

My mother came storming in, "Tom, what are you doing. He's just a child. Why are you beating him?" She pushed him to little avail as he turned and landed an uppercut on her chin, which caused her to stumble and fall back onto the floor.

I cried out, "Mommy. Are you okay?"

He estimated the damage and decided that it was enough and walked out of my room slamming the door and knocking my portrait of Mark Twain off its hook and crashing to the floor smashing the frame and glass to pieces. I hugged my mother and cried. She responded," It's okay, dear, it'll be okay. We'll figure something out."

"Mommy, I can't. I can't take this. He hurts me all the time. Can't we leave?"

"I don't know. I'll see if I can get some help, okay?"

"Yes, mommy. Does he hurt Jimmy also?"

"Jimmy hasn't told me yet, but I wouldn't be surprised. Your dad has a malicious and evil temper that I can't control."

"Did he hurt you?"

"Yes, Evan. Sometimes he does, but only since you were born. He was perfectly normal before you came into our lives."

I then thought again about the bathtub incident I wondered why I suddenly remembered these occurrences and dreamt about them at this time. Was this the genesis of my significant feeling for revenge? Was this the foundation of my misogyny and misanthropy? I realized that my evil was rooted in my parents' abuse. This didn't necessarily legitimize it but did gave me solace in its understanding. Thinking back, I really didn't recognize the meaning or ramifications of what she said that day. But I seem to appreciate it today. I gently stroked Maria's face and she awoke with a startle.

"Hey. It's getting late. Let's get back to the campus."

"Agree."

We hailed a cab and returned to the SC campus. We got a couple of sandwiches for dinner with two cokes, roast beef for her and turkey for me. When we retired to my room, I dialed my parents.

"Yes?"

"Hey, mom. It's Evan."

"Evan. So good to hear from you! How are you?"

"I'm great. My screenplay was accepted by Netflix and the coordinator feels we can go into production by the summer," I said excitedly.

"Evan. That is so, so wonderful. I am so proud."

"Yeah mom, thanks. Is dad there? I need to ask him something."

"Sure, one sec."

"Hello?"

"Hey, dad. It's Evan. I just told mom that my screenplay was accepted by Netflix for production. They're thinking of a film or possibly a limited series."

"Yes?"

"Well. They're sending the contract and I'll need representation. You know a lawyer and an agent. I thought you could help me find someone or lead me in the right direction."

"Why the fuck would I do that after what you've done to your mother. You ran off three thousand miles away to a different world to be on your own. You barely call her and overall, you're a little shit. So be on your own."

"What do you think I should say about you? You are the magnanimous one? You beat the living shit out of me. Why do you think I left, father? I don't know if I can, but I sure as hell will try to get you arrested for child abuse and domestic violence. I know about your beatings of mom. I witnessed them and she has witnessed your treatment of me too. So be forewarned. I think you may be in some trouble if I have any say."

"You're a fucking little pisser. You better not come home again because you may not survive to call anyone."

With that he slammed the phone. Two minutes later my mobile chimed the screen identifying my mother as the caller. I ignored it and started on my sandwich thanking Maria for helping me today and being a part of my happiness and achievement.

"De nada, dear Evan. I guess it didn't go so well with dad, eh?"

"Fuck him. I'll call Bergman and Steinfeld to help with the lawyer and agent. Scoot over here, Maria," I said climbing unto the bed and pulling her down to me.

We awoke the next morning and went to the cafeteria for breakfast. When we returned Maria started packing for her return to NY as I completed a paper for Psychology. On the drive to the airport, I was distracted and pensive. Maria noticed and inquired, but I was evasive. When we pulled up to the American Airlines terminal, I flipped the trunk, stepped out as did Maria and pulled out her luggage. As we stood and stared at each other, she asked about my state of mind. "I'm fine, not to worry," I volunteered.

"I am worried. You have it all going for you and you seem very unhappy, depressed and troubled. Please don't hold back. Tell me what's troubling you."

"Please, Maria. I'm fine." I pulled her close and kissed her.

But she perceived my reticence and distraction and asked again. But again, I was evasive. She no longer pursued her inquiry and turned and slowly wheeled her bag into the terminal. I stared at her back and returned to the car, started it but only stared straight ahead without driving away. After a few minutes, a traffic cop came by, knocked on my driver side window and yelled, "Come on, Move it. Now."

I drove off into the LA traffic, feeling a sense of dread.

On American flight 6041, Maria sat in a window seat staring out at the blue cloudless sky and shed a tear at what she thought was my ominous behavior and a possible warning sign but remained oblivious to its derivation or foundation.

Chapter 17

Quantico, Virginia is a small town in Prince William County, Virginia bordered by the Potomac River to the east and the Quantico Creek to the north. The population at the last census in 2010 was four hundred and eighty, but in spite of its hamlet like status, it has gained distinction as the site of the FBI Academy and Research Center. In addition to the FBI training center, it houses the Behavioral Analysis Unit (BAU), which is an integral component of the National Center of Analysis of Violent Crimes (NCAVC). The mission of the BAU is to provide information on the behavior of an individual who has committed violent crimes. The BAU looks at a detailed analysis of crimes at the request of state, local, federal or international agencies in order to help investigations, to aid in the profile unknown criminals and sort through criminal data to assist in solving a crime. It was created in 1997 as part of the NCAVC. One of its major benefits includes the formation of ViCAP (Violent crimes Apprehension Program), which contains a database available as a tool to all law enforcement agencies and contains multiple facts regarding violent crimes (such as rape, assault, and murder). It is maintained online to aid local law enforcement and allows for comparisons of criminal acts' patterns and details and thus evaluates patterns. Using this data base one can discern an MO for a given crime. Looking up in the glass enclosed office at the BAU in the Research Center of the Academy, Joseph Esposito, a so called "profiler" sat at his desk after sorting through multiple data sheets regarding a recent request concerning multiple gruesome killings in New York City, Los Angeles, California, and Beaumont Massachusetts, it was placed by one of his field agents, John McMaster. He was suddenly interrupted a piecing telephone chime.

"Yes? What is it?? I'm terribly busy."

"Sorry, chief it's McMaster."

"Yes?"

"I think you'll need to come out here. Another body was just discovered. Throat was slashed, raped possibly posthumously. BUT!"

"Yes. Go on"

"This one is a bit different than the others that I had sent you information on."

"I'm listening."

"The killer left no cross on the chest above the hear this time."

"All the other particulars are identical though?"

"She was an attractive female in her thirties. Her throat was slashed leaving blood everywhere. Unfortunately, he was meticulous this time and no samples are available for DNA analysis."

"I thought you said he raped her."

"Yes, I did but he must have used a condom or not ejaculated in or on her."

"So how the fuck do you know he raped her."

"That was the deduction of the medical examiner at the crime scene."

"Well, if he raped her there must be abrasions in her vagina that he shed so there must be some DNA."

"Sorry, sir, Nada. As I said he may have used a condom."

"That is bizarre. This fucking maniac goes and kills a young woman by slashing her throat, rapes her. But before he fucks, he puts on a condom? No way, Jose. Keep searching. There has got be a sample that we can extract some DNA from."

"Oh! By the way. The chick was a reporter for the LA times and recently had a byline on the Cross Killer."

"That's very interesting. Can you fax me her article?"

"Sure. It's coming right over."

"Great, let me look at it and I'll call you and when I'll fly out."

"It is imperative that you do. There is mass confusion and hysteria regarding these murders, and we have to help these guys. They seem lost."

"I hear you and understand. I'll call you later today."

"Thanks."

Esposito hung up and walked over to his fax machine and sorted through various papers until he saw Colleen Moore's article. He was struck by the intelligent organized, succinct and concise writing style. Each sentence appeared calculated, deliberate and contemplative. But what really emerged from the text were the interviews she conducted with the students. Most were standard immature thoughts describing shock, terror and distress at this grisly crime on their campus in close proximity to their own lives. But one interview especially piqued Esposito's curiosity, intellect and interest. That was of a young man, who seemed to have a grasp of the mind of a serial killer, the mind of a madman. He identified multiple psychological and historical characteristics that Esposito and his team had previously established: the child abuse, the desire to elicit fear, the hatred for authority and the enjoyment derived from the killing act. Esposito guessed that this young college student must have read extensively or…

Unfortunately, Colleen did not identify this precocious student by name, but that could indeed be a reason to go to L.A- to find him. He called McMaster back.

"Hey, John. I'm booking a flight for L.A. to arrive tomorrow evening."

"Great, looking forward to it."

Hanging up with McMaster, he then resumed his inspection of the data sheets that were sent by the Deputy Jim Martin from Beaumont, Mass. They included Amtrak schedules, ticket

purchases and stops along the Northeast corridor route from Boston to New York. He

highlighted one particular train, the one with the killing of a girl named Jennifer. He

searched the names, their embarkations, destinations and times. He found obvious candidates for further investigation. He then reexamined the Beaumont schedules and tried to match the data.

He would elicit the support of his IT team to better coordinate the data points. He hoped there

would only be a handful of names that corresponded to lighten the load of the investigation. That would surely make life easier. In addition, wouldn't it be remarkable if the name paralleled a Columbia student and further one who transferred to USC. But his enthusiasm wavered knowing full well that nothing was that simple. These investigations were hardly ever that uncomplicated. Complications always arose. Even this case has turned multifarious with the recent change in MO of the last killing. He was hardly discouraged but somewhat perplexed. In his study and profiles of serial killers, he rarely encountered anyone who altered their methods.

His studies have shown that a serial killer's MO, is usually dictated by the compulsion that drives him or her. Therefore, it rarely deviates. An obsessive compulsive rarely deviates for their routine. Since that compulsion is also what causes them to kill, they are powerless to stop it. The entire killing process and MO is ritualistic in order to satisfy the compulsion that drives him. One question did always bother him, whether a serial killer in order to elude capture can change his methods. He always felt that it would be very difficult to accomplish because like all compulsions they are very hard to eradicate or alter. But maybe this one is different. Maybe this guy is smart enough to modify his ritual.

He again thought about the article and that smart kid that Moore interviewed. This kid could very well be a suspect. His in depth understanding of the psychology of a serial killer was surely preternatural. He guessed it was possible to presume the kid had an interest in criminal acts, especially serial killers and was erudite, but the interview and the interviewee bothered him. He left the office and took a cab to Reagan International Airport for a nonstop flight to Los Angeles that his assistant had booked.

I returned to my room after dropping off Maria and stayed in bed until approximately 6pm. I buried my head in the comforter and cried. My melancholy was hardly unusual but profound, nonetheless. I couldn't wrap my head around it or understand its genesis. Was I anxious about my possible apprehension and subsequent incarceration? Was I despondent about what I had done or about to do further? Was it because of my last encounter with Maria, who I really liked and wanted to continue a relationship with? I wasn't sure but I couldn't control myself. I couldn't sleep, write or study. I didn't eat nor wanted to. All I did was stare out the window and continue to cry. Finally at midnight, I dialed Maria hoping she could be a source of comfort and possible joy. In my morose state, I didn't realize the time in New York and felt humiliated and embarrassed for calling her at that hour.

Waiting for her to answer and ambivalent about a desire for her to pick up the phone, I heard myself say, *Maria, I need you.* After the fifth tone, the line connected.

"Hello. Who is this at this hour?

"Maria. It's Evan. I am so, so sorry for calling and waking you, but I needed to talk to you."

"Evan? What is it? Are you okay?"

"No Maria. I'm not. I'm not at all."

"Have you been crying? You sound awful. What is it?"

"I'm so depressed. I was such an ass at the airport. I'm sorry."

"Hey! Evan. It's okay. I knew there was something bothering you, but you can sometimes be so remote and non-communicative. Frankly, I didn't understand it since you've got everything going for you, but I accepted it. No need to apologize."

"No, No. Maria. There is every reason to apologize. You have been great and I'm not sure that if I didn't have your voice to console me, I could even survive."

"Survive? Evan what are you saying? Evan, please get hold of yourself. You're scaring me."

"Maria. I can't. Please."

I hung up and collapsed back onto the bed, dropped the phone and cried some more. Lying there for approximately five minutes, I heard the chime of my cell phone. The lit face said *"Maria."* I let it ring and didn't answer. I buried my head to avoid hearing it and it stopped. I need to be alone. I needed to think things through on my own. After a few moments, it chimed again, I ignored it, but it persisted until the voice mail answered, *"Evan. Please pick up. Evan, please."* I thought that she obviously really cares about me and that I was a fucking fool to put her through this shit. I must have been acting out my father's abuse in a nonviolent way on this poor, sweet girl. What a piece of shit! Over the next half hour, she called back twice more and then at 4am she stopped. What a shit head I was. At least in my own mind I knew what I was doing. I wondered whether my father ever thought about what he was doing.

I didn't sleep the rest of the night, tossing and turning, intermittently sobbing and then just staring at my ceiling. I arose from the bed, walked to window and looked out at the bucolic campus bathed in the morning sun. The day would be glorious as evidenced by the sunshine, clear skies and crisp air coming through the window. I thought back to last night and the pleading of Maria and it made me miserable. To think that I treated a beautiful girl I really cared about in such an appalling manner was profane. Yes. I deserved what's going to happen to me. I looked in the bathroom mirror and said, *"I hope you're happy with yourself. You have alienated maybe the one person that can help you."*

I was now alone- an unidentified serial killer without love, without family, without a conscience and without hope. I knew that I would eventually be apprehended, and the rest of my life would surely be short. But I had to do what I had to do. I couldn't stop. The compulsions were too overwhelming. I wondered whether this mental state was permanent or only a reaction to the too many good things that had happened recently that I somehow didn't feel I warranted.

Hate thyself

I showered, dressed and decided to go to class. On my way, my cell phone chimed again. Looking at the screen, I saw the caller: The person I really wanted to speak to: *Maria* was visible on the screen.

"Hello."

"Hey it's me."

"Yeah, Maria, I'm sorry about last night I was a shit."

"Are you okay this morning?"

"Yeah, I'm okay."

"You sound awful though."

"I guess I have been a wreck lately."

"Listen, Evan. I don't know what's going on, but you need some help. Why don't you see the school psychologist? Maybe they can help you sort through whatever it is that's bothering you. Please."

"Nah. I'm fine."

"The hell you are. You have got to promise me to make an appointment today."

"I'll take it under advisement."

"Listen to me you obstinate son of a bitch. Please promise. I'll only tell you once. Otherwise, I might call your parents and tell them their son is severely depressed and suicidal."

"Don't you even think that! I can't bear their disingenuous interference."

"Evan, they're your parents."

"You just don't know. You just don't understand. Goodbye, Maria."

I hung up and continued to walk in my haze not realizing where I was going or what I was going to do or where I was going to go. I continued to walk and before I realized it, I was standing at the doorstep of the Student Heath Center. I went to the directory almost reflexively and looked for the psychologist. I walked the flight up to the offices, knocked on the door and waited. "Yes. Can I help you?" asked the receptionist.

"Yes. My name is Evan Dicks and I'd like to make an appointment with someone to talk to. I'm having depressive moods and need some help."

"Is this an emergency? Are you thinking of killing yourself?"

"I'm not entirely sure. I don't think I have nerve to do that. But I'm really not sure."

"One minute please." He picked up the phone and said, "Hey Craig. I think there's someone out here you might like to talk to."

Almost instantaneously, a tall, intelligent looking, long haired late twentyish man wearing wire framed glasses appeared. He greeted me, "Hey, I'm Craig Darby. I'm a PhD candidate in psychology. Please follow me."

"Evan Dicks," I replied and followed him to an office in the back of the suite.

He sat in a swivel chair in front of the desk and pointed to an armchair next to him. "Please. Sit"

"Charles, my assistant said you're feeling blue and have suicidal thoughts?"

Surprisingly I replied, "I never said that, but I am feeling low."

"I guess he can be a bit dramatic. How long have you been feeling this way?"

"It's a relatively recent feeling. Up until this week everything was going absolutely great for me. "I recently moved to USC from Columbia to pursue a career in screenwriting. I'm enrolled in the SCA." "Ah, the School of Cinematic Arts. Yes, I know it well. It's the best in the country."

"Yes. That's what I'm told. Anyway, I wrote a screenplay as a treatment of a novel for a writing class final at Columbia. My English professor loved it and sent it to the content and talent coordinator at

Netflix and they've decided to produce it. Somehow and paradoxically, this all has depressed me. I'm not feeling worthy and have been having these thoughts of hating myself, I'm, having difficulty writing sleeping and even conversing with my girlfriend." Darby listened, took notes but didn't say a word while I continued.

"My girlfriend suggested I speak to the school's psychologist but instead of agreeing, I verbally attacked her and hung up on her. Next thing I realized after aimlessly walking towards class, I ended up here."

"How old did you say you were?"

"I didn't but I'm nineteen, nearly twenty."

"You know. On a superficial level, one would believe that you have absolutely nothing to be depressed about, at least based on that story, but obviously there's more here below the surface. Tell me about what you do besides school here at USC. Do you have any friends? Do you have any outside interests besides school and writing? You did mention a girlfriend? But first tell me a little more about you as an individual."

"Where do I begin? I was born and raised in Beaumont, Massachusetts by I guess two less than loving parents. I never had many friends while growing up or in high school. I guess I was kind of a loner. Interestingly, when I started college, I gained assurance and confidence and did start dating and had a couple of girlfriends over the past few months."

"Yes. You mentioned that a girlfriend suggested you speak to us."

"Yes. Maria, she is absolutely great."

"Have you spoken to her about your mood?"

"I have but it seems useless. There are just too many thoughts swimming around in my head to explore with her."

"Do you feel like you can explore them here?"

"I'm not sure but I guess I'll have to try. Agree?"

"Sorry, that's not for me to say."

"Uh huh. Typical shrink talk."

"Sorry. I think we'll have to pick this up next week. I have another appointment."

"Understood. Thank you."

I arose from the comfortable armchair, shook his hand and walked out the door. He patted me on my back. "Please come back, Evan. I think I can help you."

Walking down the flight of stairs and through the front door, I felt little difference. But I did understand that speaking to this student was not such a bad idea. After all, we only spent thirty-five minutes with each other. So, what did I expect? I decided that I would apologize to Maria and let her know that I took her advice and would be undergoing counselling. I thought she would be happy about that.

"Hey, Maria. It's Evan."

"Evan. You sound better."

"Hardly but I did go to the health center and am seeing a counsellor, a PhD candidate in psychology."

"Boy. That's great Evan. I'm so glad and relieved."

"Thanks, Maria. Thank you for insisting on that. I believe that it may be helpful. Maybe it'll help understand some things about who I am and my psyche. Thanks again and I'll see ya!"

Chapter 18

Detective Alexandra Saunders had the weekend off, so she decided to drive up to Beaumont to see Captree. They had been communicating over these past few months but hadn't seen each other since the abduction of his daughter, Claudia and the investigation into the Amtrak murder. The drive to Massachusetts was pleasant since she took the Cross Sound Ferry from Orient Point, Long Island to New London, Connecticut. That detour cut miles of traffic and the ferry ride allowed her to continue to work and study the data that Captree and his deputy, Martin had sent her. She was very disappointed that the investigation hadn't produced a viable suspect as of yet, but she was very pleased to go see Captree. She was attracted to him. He was good-looking, a good father and a genuinely nice guy. The hundred and twenty miles from New London to Beaumont was an easy ride with little traffic or stoppage. When she reached Beaumont, she went directly to the Sherriff's office. Even though it was Saturday as she knew Captree would be there working. She hoped to surprise him. Walking into the small non-descript office, she met a deputy at the front desk.

"Yes. May I help you?" the desk sergeant said to the attractive sophisticated appearing woman standing next to him. He was used to that kind of persona in Beaumont but hardly ever in the sheriff's office.

"I'm looking for Captain Captree."

"Captree, huh? Not for yours truly, Sgt. Mitman, eh?"

"No. I'm afraid not. Is Captree here?"

"Yes. I'll get him."

With that he arose went to the back of the office and returned with Ronald Captree. As soon as he saw her, he ran over and gave her a bear-like hug.

"Alex!! What are you doing here?" Why didn't you tell me you were coming? I would have prepared and made plans."

"I wanted to surprise you."

Meanwhile Mitman looked on in amazement at the good fortune of this Captree. He shook his head muttering unintelligently and sat back down at his desk.

"Wait right there. I'll get my coat and we'll get some lunch. Boy, is it good to see you," he said shaking his head in disbelief. While Captree was away, Sgt Mitman asked, "How do you two know each other?"

"Ron and I met in New York when he came down to investigate the murder you had up here. You remember that high school girl who was raped and slaughtered. He came down to New York because we had three others that were very similar to that one."

"Ah, yes. Emily O'Connor. We still don't have many clues on that one. Anything on the others?"

"Not really, except there were three others in California and the FBI has just sent its BAU team to Los Angeles."

BAU?"

"Behavioral Analysis Unit. You know, those hot shot "profilers."

"Got ya."

Captree re-emerged form the back grabbed Saunders' hand and they walked out. Mitman sat at the desk continuing to shake his head. He was not sure the reason for that - his misfortune or Captree's good fortune. They walked the two blocks to the Blue Mountain Café and sat at a window table. He ordered a cheeseburger, which he claimed was the best in town with a Coke, and she ordered the Cobb Salad with an iced tea.

"So, why did you really come to Beaumont today."

"The truth? Or subterfuge?"

"Let me hear the story first."

"I really came to discuss the Cross Killer. I have some ideas that may be helpful," she replied.

"And the verisimilitude?"

She blushed and admitted, "To see you again."

"That's great because I've missed you, too. I think we have plenty of time to talk about the case. I can take the rest of the day off so let's go for a ride and enjoy the day."

They finished their lunch, left and got into her car. They drove down Main Street and headed for the local arboretum. When they stopped, he sidled over to the driver's side, touched her cheek with a sly smile on his face. He grabbed her chin, turned it towards him and kissed her passionately. She returned his kiss and they hugged for nearly a minute.

"Hey. It is really good to see you," Captree exclaimed.

"I am so glad to be here. I've missed male companionship for a long while now."

"So have I."

"Male companionship?" she asked quizzically and laughingly.

"Yeah!" he responded with amusement.

They spent the weekend together with nary a mention of the Cross Killer or the brilliant ideas she claimed she had.

I found my way to the Health Center the following week for Interview #2 with my new therapist, the PhD student, Darby.

As I walked into his office he greeted me, "Good morning, Evan, how you doing?"

"About the same. No major change."

"So where were we?" Looking at his notes he said, "Ah, yes we were talking about Maria. Have you spoken to her?

"Yes. We've spoken," I replied.

"Did you mention our discussion?"

"Not in so many words."

"You did say that she has been a willing for you, did you bring up you issues with her?"

"I really didn't mention my mood or depression to her, but I assume she could infer there was

something bothering by my voice and aloof manner and attitude."

"You mean you actually displayed that?"

"I think so."

"She didn't inquire about it though?"

"Yeah, she did, but I was very enigmatic."

"Okay, have you been able to talk to anyone else about your feelings?"

"I really don't have many other friends or acquaintances here in L.A yet."

"What about your parents?"

"I'd rather not talk about them."

"Hmm. Why not?"

"I said that I don't want to discuss my parents."

"Don't you feel you can go to them with problems?"

"No. I don't. Please let's stop this conversation."

"You know in order to do behavioral modification to help depression you have to find a comfort zone to explore. It can be friends, close acquaintances or parents but someone must be supportive, to help you regain confidence."

"My parents are hardly that supportive possibility. Matter of fact, I hardly ever speak to them."

"Why is that?"

"It just is."

"Tell me. What are they like? Did you have a good relationship with them when you were in high school? What about as a child" Were thing better then? Do you have any siblings? Do they feel the same way that you do?"

I responded to this repetitive inquiry with indignation, "Hey, I said I didn't want to discuss my parents or my siblings or my home life. If you can't skip this inquisition, we'll have to stop right now."

"No. I'm sorry. Please don't get angry with me. I'm trying to help you."

"Okay, go on."

"What do think is making you so sad? Are you feeling especially anxious?"

"Not really but I do have my moments of extreme anxiety, but they are rare."

"Tell me about school. How is that going? How are your grades?"

"I'm doing okay."

"Listen. You don't seem to want to talk much today. Why don't we pick this up next week?"

When I heard that comment I grew very anxious and morose. "I really would like to talk some more if you don't mind and if you have the time."

"Okay."

I needed to extricate myself from my deep inner thoughts and pain and emotion, so I decided to broach the subject he was anxious to discuss, "My parents are awful. My dad beats the shit out of me, my mother and my brother. My mother abused me as a child until I was ten or eleven. My father beats my mother also. My brother, James is a good kid, and he was verbally abused that I could hear. I'm not sure about physical abuse, though."

Craig Darby sat there with his mouth agape at what he was hearing. He didn't expect this flood of emotion and it showed. He didn't know what to say or do, "My oh my. Did you ever report them?"

"No. I haven't. But I have been thinking about it."

"You know! I'm going to have to by law if what you're saying is really true."

"Crap. You don't believe me after nearly pleading for me to tell you about my home life.

That is just great. Thanks for nothing and this wonderful intervention."

"Hey, man. Relax."

I got up and ran out of the office and started crying. Tears were streaming down my face as I bolted down the stairs and out the front door. I nearly ran over a student walking into the center, excused myself and kept running to my dorm room. When I finally reached the room, I collapsed on the bed and thought about the consequences of my confession.

"*What have I done?*

I just painted a red flag on my chest. I've opened myself to an investigation. Why did I do such a stupid thing? What was I thinking? Better yet. Why wasn't I thinking? It was as if I was in an outer body experience. How did that son of a bitch dupe into such a ridiculous conversation? Evan you're smarter than that. Maybe not, I thought to myself.

I decided maybe Maria could help me. I dialed her number. Unfortunately, her voice mail responded, *"Hi. You've reached Maria. Sorry. I can't answer right now. Please leave your name and number and I'll get back to you as soon as I can."*

Hi, Maria, It's Evan. Please call me. I need to speak to you as soon as possible.

I closed my eyes and fell asleep.

Chapter 19

The crime scene at the Moore murder was cordoned off when Esposito arrived. He was met there by McMaster, and they entered the apartment together. The shocking scene surprised McMaster but not Esposito as he had seen many a serial killer crime scene like this in his ten years in the Bureau. He walked into the bedroom to a panorama of blood everywhere-on the floors, on the walls, even a spot on the eight-foot ceiling, probably evidence of the carotid artery having been severed. The body of Colleen Moore had been removed. Esposito searched the room, the bed, the sheets and pillows. He looked at her desk, computer, desk drawers and her dresser. He bent down and carefully inspected the carpet and finally the door. He searched for clues in the living area and kitchen. Unfortunately, there was no evidence of a second person having been there. There were no dirty glasses, empty cartons, or garbage. Whoever did this really cleaned out the place efficiently and surprisingly professionally? He would have thought that the killer would be very anxious to leave the premises as soon as possible rather than clean the place so carefully.

"A most fastidious fellow, wouldn't you say," Esposito said to no one in particular.

"Indeed," commented McMaster.

"Did someone inspect the garbage downstairs?" asked Esposito.

"Yes", said McMaster. "The LAPD said that they found nothing."

"We'll go down soon and look again, but first I'd like to take another look around here."

Esposito went back into the bedroom and inspected every inch of the bed, which turned up nothing. He bent down on all fours and carefully looked at the floor. McMaster thought he was with Sherlock Holmes watching the degree of care he took with his examination. Esposito even used a magnifying glass for completeness. To McMaster's astonishment, Esposito arose with a three-inch-long strand of brown hair.

"Hey. Sherlock, where's the pipe? "McMaster asked jokingly.

"In my back pocket, shmuck. Let's go. We have got to get this to the lab ASAP for DNA analysis. Even though I suspect that this killer is the same as the Cross Killer. This will verify it. Thus, he must be in L.A. at present. She was a reporter and interviewed a bunch of students regarding the previous murder so we can at least canvas the university and try to find out who she spoke to. One especially interesting interview was the one with that kid that seemed to know everything about the psychology of a serial killer. Maybe he's in the Psych department. Well at least there are some leads."

"Yes. Good job but I wouldn't have expected anything lesser from the country's chief profiler," said McMaster.

"Stop wit that crap. There is no job description in the Bureau as a "profiler". We're behaviorists with an interest in the mind of the serial killer. Understand?"

"Yes sir."

They left the apartment heading back to the LAPD South District office.

"Hello."

"Hey, Evan, It's Maria. What's up? You sounded awful on the phone."

"Yeah, Sorry. I'm a wreck. I don't know what it is but I'm so down. When can you come back?"

"I don't know, Ev. I don't have that kind of money and school doesn't end until the end of the month and then there are two weeks of finals."

"Yeah, shit."

"Don't you have finals too?"

"Yeah, but I don't seem to give a shit."

"What? Evan. That doesn't sound like you at all."

"Yeah. I guess. I got to go. I'll e-mail you. Bye."

"Wait. Don't hang up yet."

"Okay. What can I do for you?"

"Evan. You're the one that sounds like they're in trouble. What can I do to help you?"

"I can't understand what is driving these blues, but I can't seem to shake it. The school psychologist was hardly helpful, but I think I'll go back again. I saw him twice and things became dicey when we discussed my parents."

"That's not surprising."

"Yeah. We also discussed you. He suggested I should seek your assistance in behavior modification. What do you think? Do you think you can help modify my behavior? Obviously, it's distorted and twisted. Don't you think I need to straighten it out," I remarked facetiously.

"Sorry, Evan, I don't understand what you're talking about."

"Sorry. It's hard for me to explain right now. But someday you may very well understand."

"Huh? When? What the hell do you mean?"

"You'll see. Someday, maybe soon, all this will become very clear and understandable."

"You're not only talking about your depression and blues? Are you, Ev? You're talking about something bigger and seemingly more portentous? Aren't you? Evan, you're really scaring me. What exactly have you done or contemplating?"

"No. Nothing. Forget it. Everything is fine. I'm sorry that I even mentioned it. We'll talk soon, okay and please don't worry."

"Easier said than done considering how I feel about."

Yeah, thanks, so long dear one, speak to you soon.

I hung up and lied back on the bed and shed more tears until I fell asleep.

Captree was flat on his back thinking about his recent encounter with Alexandra Saunders. They did do some work eventually. They were able to compare the names on the Amtrak train with those of the ticketed passengers on the Beaumont train to Boston. One name stood out. He would have to research this one individual further. At least it was a lead.

But now the more pressing thought was how to tell this lovely woman, Sarah Dicks, at his side the truth. He had been seeing her for approximately six months, but he knew it couldn't last and would have to cease. She was married and thus, this presented complications that first needed to be resolved. He felt he could make it work, especially given her unhappiness with her belligerent abusive husband. But now another impediment became evident, Alexandra Saunders. He brushed Sarah's hair and gently kissed her cheek to wake her. He stated her lovely biblical name, Sarah. She stirred and he looked at her. He observed the beautiful bedroom in this expansive house and wondered how she ended up with this maniac. The stories she told him were harrowing. She related the numerous verbal and physical abuses of her son. She also shared his abuse of her. She had tried numerous times to report him, but he always seemed to parry her with kind words of apology and forgiveness. She was like most abused spouses in domestic violent relationships, blaming her own shortcomings for the abuse. Captree had tried to help her with encouraging reinforcement and the positivity of their relationship, which was the one of the optimistic aspects of their relationship. When he suggested that Tom Dicks should be indicted, she demurred and refused to press charges. But now he had to end it for his and her benefit. Would she understand? He feared her reaction. He touched her face again and slowly bent down to kiss her when he heard the bedroom door crash in. Thomas Dicks stormed in with a Barretta M1951 blazing and shouting, "You fuckin whore. "He fired and hit Sarah Dicks in the head as she arose from her slumber. He fired a second shot and hit Captree. Then he turned the gun toward his temple and fired a third shot. Captree fell back and gasped. Blood splattered all over the bedroom's pale gray carpet and the off-white wall turning it a dripping crimson. Captree gasped again, touching his chest which was bleeding profusely. He was able to gather the strength to dial 911 on his cell phone and then collapsed as he fell back saying, "Help the Dicks home."

By the time the sheriff's office arrived, Captree was barely breathing with only a faint pulse. An ambulance was able to get him to Beaumont Hospital. The Emergency Room team worked on him for almost two hours, before they were able to stabilize his vital signs and get him to the OR. Jim Martin was the first one on the scene at the Dicks' home. He secured the crime scene and then searched for survivors in the rest of the house. No one else was present or hurt. So, he called the middle school to get James to the principal's office explaining the circumstances in vague terms. He then searched for other possible family members listed in Sarah Dicks' directory. He found a sister and called her with the tragic news. She lived in Boston and confirmed that she would drive to Beaumont immediately.

Judith Baylor arrived at the sheriff's office within the hour and rushed into the waiting area and inquired about the Dicks shooting. She was accompanied to Martin's office and saw James Dicks who was sitting with his head in his hands, distraught, disheveled and crying. She ran over to his side, hugged his head saying, "Jimmy. Are you okay?"

"Yes, Aunt Judy, I'm fine. Did you hear what happened? Mommy is dead. Daddy shot her."

"Yes. I heard. I'm so, so sorry, Jimmy. You'll come home with me."

"What about Evan?"

"I'll call him as soon as I can."

At that moment Martin interrupted the conversation, "Thank you so much for coming so rapidly. My partner is at Beaumont Hospital in surgery, and I have to get over there."

"Is there anything you can tell me?"

"Sorry. I don't know much. It looks like your brother-in law found your sister and Capt. Captree in bed together and he shot them both and then fired a bullet into his temple. Did you know your sister and my partner were having an affair? Did she ever reveal any details about that?"

"No. I didn't know. She never spoke about an extramarital affair. She was rather insular and was laconic about her private life. Although, I did know she was having some problems with Tom, her husband."

"Yes. That's what I heard, too. Capt. Captree had mentioned abuse. Did you know that was going on?'

"No, sorry, I hadn't heard about that. Jimmy, did your daddy ever hit your mommy?"

James Dicks looked at his aunt sheepishly and whispered as if hoping no one would or could hear, "Yes, Aunt Judy, he hit mommy, Evan and me." He hit us many, many times, but mommy always said that it would stop. She said that she would protect us and take care of it, but she never did. He put his head in his hands again and cried uncontrollably. Judy Baylor hugged him and desperately tried to comfort him. She looked at Sgt. Martin in disbelief and proclaimed definitively, "I had no idea. This is truly astonishing. I guess his anger was insurmountable and he finally snapped when he saw her with your partner."

"Yeah. I guess. What surprises me is that Captree had this clandestine affair. It really doesn't sound like him"

"I suppose you don't know my sister. She is a very attractive and persuasive woman. I would think she is hard to resist and was the initiator."

"I think you probably ought to call your other nephew. Evan?"

"Yes. I'll call him immediately."

"Cut!" exclaimed the director sitting in front of a Sony F-55 camera equipped with Zeiss Ultra prime lenses with a 19-90 Fujinon zoom. That camera and lens combination is chosen by many Netflix directors because of the quality of the image and the Netflix 4K requirement. "That was good, but the dialog needs some work. Hey, Dicks, we need more authoritative dialog here. Work on that this evening. Okay?"

Evan looked at J. Paul Bradley, the author of the novel, who was also there in the studio for the shooting and replied, "Sure. I'll work on it tonight. No problem."

"Okay! Set up the next scene. Let's go. We haven't got all day. Time is money and we're on a strict budget here."

Evan was not shocked by the directness or brusque manner of this director as he was known as a perfectionist who was very tough on his crew but was also had won two Emmys and considered one of the best. The showrunner and producer walked over to Evan and comforted him, "Not to worry, kid. He doesn't mean anything by it. Deep down, he's a real sweetheart."

"Thanks," he said and then spoke to Bradley about the changes in the dialog that he thought could please the director. Bradley, having gotten some vacation time from his hospital duties, agreed to meet in the trailer after the day's shooting to improve he dialog and draft the necessary changes.

As the new scene unfolded, Evan heard his cell chime. He tried to ignore it, but its persistent ring grew interruptive and bothersome, so he finally answered after hanging up the first three times.

"Yes? This is Evan Dicks."

"Evan!" responded the voice. "It's Judy."

"Judy?"

"Yes, it's Aunt Judith from Boston."

"Aunt Judy? What is it? Why are you calling me? You never do."

"I know. Sorry. Something awful has happened, and you need to come home on the next plane out of Los Angeles!"

"What happened? I'm in the middle of shooting the Netflix series of my screenplay."

"Yes. Your mom mentioned that to me but I'm sorry that will have to wait for the time being.

"What the hell is it? What happened?"

"I'm so sorry to have to tell you this, but your mom and dad are dead. Your dad killed her and shot the man she was with and then killed himself."

In shock, Evan dropped his phone and collapsed on the nearest chair. He gathered himself, picked up the phone and exclaimed, "My God. Mom is gone, Dad is dead. Shit! Is Jimmy, okay?"

"Yes. Here's here with me right now. We'll be going to Boston to my home. You can come there. I'll start arranging the funeral and help you anyway I can."

There was silence on the other end. "Evan? Are you there? Are you okay?"

"Yes, I'm here. No, I'm not okay. How could I be hearing this? Let me say hello to Jimmy. Hi. Jimmy. Hang in there, kid. I'm coming home and I'll see you tomorrow, okay?"

He heard the whimpering of his brother, "Mommy and Daddy are dead. Evan, what are we going to do?"

"We'll figure it out. Don't worry. I'll take care of you," I answered though I had no idea what I could do.

His aunt was kind and supportive, but she had a life of her own with her wife and I wasn't sure they really wanted or could accept a young teen to take care of. Aunt Judy, whenever questioned, had always proclaimed to his mom that she never wanted children and had a full life without them. Meanwhile, I had to get back to L.A. for the filming and the necessary re-writes. I was mostly working remotely and trying to accommodate the demanding and discontented director, which at times was very challenging. Sometimes, I needed the experienced voice of Professor Bergman to deliberate concepts, and he was very helpful, but I felt I needed to be present for the filming to better grasp what the director was searching for. So, I felt conflicted and anxious about this turn of events. Of interest to me, was the lack of melancholy and sorrow I should have been feeling at the death of my parents. But I did note the turmoil present in Jimmy.

I spent an entire week with Aunt Judy and her wife, Cleo and Jimmy. To clear my head, I roamed the streets at night, just strolling, meeting strangers at music clubs and coffee houses, going to movies. The night before I was going to leave Boston, I met a Generation Z'er, a mid-twenties female with attitude, in a local music club, known for heavy rock music. I was standing on the dance floor about a hundred feet from the stage, drinking a club soda with lime and listening to the ear shattering music when I felt a tap on my shoulder.

"Hey, move over. I need some space."

"Yeah, right. And where am I going to move to?"

"That's not really my problem, is it?"

"I guess not, but as you can see it's not mine either."

We were shouting over the music and conversation was impossible so I suggested there would be more elbow space outside and asked if she would like to join me. She looked perplexed but intrigued. Gave me the once over and then stared at me again. She then grabbed my hand and said, "Let's get out of here, okay?"

Her name was Julie Simpson. She was an archetypal Generation Z'er, working at Twitter in Boston, unmarried, unattached and hardly interested in either. She was attractive in a subtle not beautiful way with a gregarious personality exuding extreme confidence. In conversation, he remarked that she was a strong proponent of BLM, legalization of marijuana, and pro-choice. When out conversation turned personal, she admitted that she was bisexual and although had a strong libido, her sex life was sporadic. Hearing this, my ears perked up and that "feeling" again percolated in my being. Continuing the conversation, she precipitously suggested that we depart to her apartment. In shock at the unexpectedness of the request, I readily accepted.

"Great, I don't live far from her," she said as she grabbed my hand.

"I thought I saw some people you were talking to. Didn't you come here with them?"

"Not to worry. They won't miss me at all."

We walked the half of dozen blocks to her modern high rise on Canal Street. We entered the elevator and rode up to the eighth floor. I noted that there was no doorman. Thus, I inquired, "This is a fancy shmansy building. Why no doorman?"

"Yes, there usually is. He must be on a break."

I noted this and knew that I would have to be especially careful upon departing the building. We entered the one-bedroom corner apartment with a panoramic view of the Charles River.

I remarked, "Hey, this is really a nice place. Thanks for inviting me."

"How old did you say you were, Evan?"

"Nearly twenty but very mature for my age," I said with a chuckle.

"Yes. I bet you are."

I looked at her closely not clearly understanding her meaning. "So, tell me about this series that you're working on. It's amazing that at your age you were able to sell a screenplay to Netflix.

I related the plot of "Deadly Motivations" and thanked her for the compliment.

"Can I get you a drink?"

"Sure. Do you have any beer?"

"Of course, make yourself comfortable and I'll go get it."

I sat on the leather couch facing the window and perused a copy of "New". When she returned with two imported Belgium pilsners and some chips and an avocado dipping sauce, I remarked that I had interned at "New" that summer and she responded, "Honestly? That's a great tech magazine. You must be a bright guy."

"Not really. I was lucky getting that gig."

"I thought you go to USC?"

"I do now. I enrolled at Columbia first but transferred when Netflix wanted to film 'Deadly Motivations.'"

"Amazing, I still don't believe that you at your age and lack of experience, you were able to sell a script."

Not knowing how to respond, I merely stared out the window and said matter-of-factly. "Gorgeous view."

"Yes, it is. I love Boston."

"Did you go to school here?" I asked.

"Yes, I graduated MIT with a BS in Computer Science."

"And I'm the bright kid?"

She stood, walked to the window and suggested, "Come here. I want to point something out."

I walked over to the window, and she pointed across the Charles River to the MIT campus and said, "Right there is MIT and there is Harvard Square."

I acknowledged the geography and said, "I applied to Harvard but unfortunately didn't get in."

"You're not the only one, smart ass," she continued.

We sat back on the couch finished our beers and I stated, "I guess I better get going. I have an early flight to California tomorrow."

"What the fuck. Did you really think that invited you just for a beer?"

She then cozied up to me, grabbed my chin and kissed my cheek. Then she kissed me on the mouth, and I felt her tremble. I kissed her back, cupped her breast and she moaned. I then touched her thigh and worked my had down her jeans and rubbed her vagina. She responded with a mild groan, pulled me up from the couch and pulled me toward the bedroom. I followed her as I was taking my shirt off. She pushed me onto the bed and stood over me removing her hooded shirt revealing her breasts. She then joined me on the bed and unbuttoned my jeans and touched my erect penis. That irresistible urge again declared itself and my mind wavered. *Did I want to harm this sweet woman? I knew the rejoinder. Yes. I do. But why? My father's verbal abuse entered my brain and declared itself. Yes, yes you do you piece of shit.* I then heard my mother's disingenuous cajoling. *No, Evan. No. Mommy will protect you. Don't worry, please don't worry.* The confusion didn't last long because I knew what I had to do: that "urge," that "feeing," would not allow me to not do what I had to do. It would not allow me to stop.

"Evan, what is it?" Julie asked at my hesitancy. I removed her panties and she moaned.

"Nothing. I'm good," I said.

As she turned to straddle me, I found the knife in my pants and slashed he throat. The sight of her terror and her gasp caused me to orgasm instantaneously. I slashed her five more times across her face, chest, abdomen and limbs. She groaned and fell back with the horror remaining on her lifeless face. Resigning myself to the inevitable and thinking about my dead father, his abuse and my sexually deviant mother and their views on religion, I carved the cross over her heart. Trying to punish her further for being a woman, I entered her before I left the apartment and climaxed again. I cleaned myself off, checked for self-identifying markers, cleared the glasses and empty beer bottled and headed for the stairwell with the bag of garbage I had collected. I opened the door, searched for the doorman and was able to avoid him on my way out of the lobby. I walked down Canal Street to the T. The streets were fairly crowded for a Thursday evening, but I was just a young student heading home, so no one questioned my presence. When I reached Aunt Judy's apartment, I noted Jimmy watching TV and asked, "Where is Aunt Judy and Cleo?"

"They went out to dinner?"

"What and left you here by yourself?"

"No. I told them to go. I'm not very hungry."

"You sure? Can I get you something from the deli for you?"

"No thanks, Ev. I'm good."

I accepted his refusal, went to the bedroom and finished packing. The following morning, at 7am I greeted James, Judy and Cleo sitting at the kitchen table having breakfast.

"Well, I'm off. I'm going back to L.A."

"Are you sure? You can stay as long as you'd like," suggested Judith.

"No. I have to get back, but I am going to stop off in N.Y first to see my girlfriend. Thank you very much Aunt Judy. And thanks for helping out with Jimmy."

"Hey, Evan I'm so sorry. If you need anything, please call. You be careful, okay?"

"Thanks. I'll call when I get back to California."

"That would be great."

I walked over to James, gave him a bear hug and tearfully said, "Bye, Bro," and walked out.

At 11am, within the din of the third floor of the Boston Twitter offices sat Imani Moss, disquieted and concerned. It was not like Julie not to show up at work or answer her persistent calls. Imani, Julie Simpson's sometimes lover and fellow engineer at Twitter was a pretty, early twenties Black female. She and Julie were working on a new algorithm on data processing for Twitter, and today was to be an important code writing one. Without Julie's mastery of code, the exercise would be futile, so Imani kept calling and texting with no response. She decided to return to a different project and try again later in the day. She wondered if Julie had forgotten their dinner date also. At 6pm, Imani left the office for the Japanese restaurant, where they had arranged to meet. She sat at one of the cubicles, washed her hands with the warm towel and sipped cold sake. After two hours, having been stood up, she paid the check for her drink and decided, after again receiving no response to her calls or texts, to visit her apartment. She knocked forcefully and rang the bell multiple times to no avail. Her concern and apprehension grew more, but what could she do? She left and spent a restless night worrying about her friend. By 10am the next day she still had not contacted her, so she decided to call the Boston Police Department.

"Hello, my name is Imani Moss and I'd like to report a missing person."

"How long has this person been missing?" asked the receptionist answering the call.

"At least twenty-four hours."

"Well. Where are you? Can you come to the station In District A-1?"

Imani Moss spent the next three hours describing Julie Simpson, their relationship, their workplace environment and Julie's gregarious personality. She gave the sergeant, Julie's address, apartment number and phone number as well as her own contact information.

"Thank you, Ms. Moss. We'll be in touch was the curt farewell offered by the sergeant.

Asking the doorman for access to the apartment, the sergeant and his partner entered a scene straight out of "Friday the 13th." They called the Homicide division detective, the medical examiner, and the crime scene investigator. By the time the detectives retuned to the office, there was already a dossier on the crime and a printout of a database detailing the Cross Killer's previous murders. They contacted the FBI Behavioral Analysis Unit and were contacted by Agent Esposito a short time later.

Sitting on the Boston to New York Acela, I was completely lost in my laptop and recent script addition that needed to be completed by the next morning 6am PDT.

"Evan! Evan Dicks, is that you?"

I continued to work as if not hearing the high-pitched female voice.

"Hey. Come on, it's me Beth, Beth Murray. You remember."

I looked up and standing there was a classmate from Beaumont High. Beth was one of the Emily's very good friends and a member of the same clique that had always ignored me.

"Ah, yes, Beth. It's nice to see you."

"Look at you. You have remarkably changed-wire rims, longish hair, pronounced stubble and an air of confidence in your voice. What happened to that nerd from Beaumont?" she asked.

I looked at her without responding, when pointing to the seat next to me she asked, "Mind if I sit down?"

"Well," I said hesitatingly, "I have a shitload of work to do."

"Not to worry. I won't bother you at all. I'll be as quiet as a sleeping baby."

Knowing that that was hardly possible with Beth Murray I unsettlingly, nevertheless responded, "Suit yourself."

She sat next to me and not a moment passed before she asked, "What are you working on?"

I immediately knew that finishing the additional script alterations would be futile in face of this gabbing girl, so I closed the laptop and said, "So tell me, how have you been?"

"Great. I'm going to New York to check out NYU."

"Weren't you going to Tufts?"

"Yes. But I decided to transfer to a New York school. Boston and Beaumont bring back terrible memories and are too depressing for me. I just couldn't purge those feelings over these past months."

"I understand. Thinking about Emily, huh?"

"Yes, that was horrible, gruesome. It was so awful. Poor Em! You know, they have yet to find the killer. Isn't that unbelievable? Unfortunately, I heard about your folks. How are you holding up? I'm so sorry for your loss. Your dad went crazy, huh?"

"Yeah, thanks. I feel real bad for my brother, Jimmy. He's now all alone. I recently transferred from Columbia to the USC Film School. As a matter of fact, I was working on a screenplay when you interrupted me."

"A screenplay? Wow."

"Yeah, Netflix is producing it and I was busy with some additions."

"Holy shit, that is fantastic. No wonder you seem so confident and different. How did my friends and I not know this about you? We were surely a bunch of asses for disregarding you all those years. If you live in California, why are you headed to New York?"

"I'm stopping off to visit my girlfriend at Columbia and then heading back to L.A tomorrow morning. I was in Boston with my Aunt Judy, who is taking care of Jimmy. We were in Beaumont for the funeral. I have too much to do to hang around. I have to get back to the filming and the constant re-writes at the behest of the director."

"So, no time to have lunch or dinner with an old friend, I guess?"

"Sorry, not really. Maybe we can get together some other time."

"That would be great. Here is my cell number."

Our conversation was longer than it seemed and as we pulled into Penn Station, she handed me her cell number with an inviting smile. I looked back at her and returned her glaze and said, "So long, Beth. Nice seeing and speaking to you again."

"Indeed, Evan."

I left the train, waved good-bye to Beth and walked quickly toward the stairs leading to 7th Avenue. On 7th Avenue, I took a cab to Maria's dorm room , she had recently moved onto campus. Maria answered the door with a rather forlorn and quizzical look when she saw me.

"Hey. What are you doing here?"

I walked into the room and said, "I told you I was coming down from Boston as soon as I was able to get my shit together."

"I guess. But I didn't expect it would be this soon. I expected that you would stay in Boston a while longer with your aunt and brother. Are you okay? Man. I can't conceive of the shock and grief you must be experiencing. The last time we spoke you seemed really out of it. Now with this on top of what seemed like your depression, you must really be hurting. Has your therapist helped you? Have you spoken to him about your parents? Tell me, please that you're all right.

I looked at her and tried to mollify her. "Listen. I was a shit. I had a very depressive couple of weeks. I'm not sure why. Maybe the success of the screenplay and "too much too soon" was what I couldn't tolerate. I am really sorry. I do like you and want us to be good. But now with this suicide of my father and the killing of my mom, I definitely need some time."

She searched my eyes for honesty, and I presume she found it as she said, "Hey. It's fine. I understand. We're good. Believe me."

"Thanks, Maria."

I pulled her closer and hugged her and then kissed her, which she returned willingly. I sat on her bed while she remained standing, and I pulled her down, but she resisted. "No. Not now. You just said you need time. Well, I need time too. We need to talk more about what exactly is going on in your head."

"I told you."

"Sorry. Not good enough. You frightened me and you didn't make much sense. It was if I was speaking to a total stranger, someone that I hadn't been with or even known."

We spent the rest of the evening discussing my feelings, my insecurities and my fears. I'm not sure whether she was able to ascertain the true reasons for my depression, my "other life", my "fears of capture" or my insecurities, my inability to stop my dark persona form its goal. We spoke into the night. At 8pm I suggested that I had to get to JFK to catch the red eye to L.A. She acknowledged and said, "Evan, I do like you also but I'm just not sure we should continue seeing each other. Anyway, you're in sunny California and I'm in dark, cold depressing, New York, so I agree, maybe this is as good a reason as any to cool it for a while."

I looked at her somewhat perplexed but obviously recognizing all she was saying and concurred. "You might be right but please, do me a favor, talk to me when I call and help me if I ask and be there for me."

"Evan, I can't believe you're feeling that insecure. You have grown so much since we first met and have gained so much confidence. I still think there is more to the story than you're letting on, but I will indeed be there for you. Don't worry."

I shrugged and gave her another hug., grabbed my bag, went out the front door and said, "Buenas noches, mi querido."

"Hey, your Spanish is really improving, *my dear,* see ya"

I walked out the building, hailed a cab and looked back at Columbia thinking that it might be the last time I see that campus or Maria.

PART THREE
CONFESSION

There is no refuge from confession but suicide; and suicide is confession.

-Daniel Webster

Chapter 20

Alexandra Saunders sat in the ICU of Beaumont Community Hospital staring at the man she had bedded just a short time ago. He was on a ventilator with electrodes attached to his chest leading to a heart monitor with continuous and disturbing beeps loudly heard throughout the room and the entire floor. He was in a coma and had been according to his thoracic surgeon since his eight-hour open heart surgery to repair the damage to his lungs, heart and ascending aorta. She was told he was barely alive when they opened him and needed nearly a transfusion of his entire blood volume to resuscitate him. She sat there conflicted. The details of his shooting were disturbing and confusing. He was found in bed with a married woman, whose husband in a fit of rage shot her, the man, Captree, and himself in a gruesome murder/suicide. Next to the bed in deep silence and obvious anguish was a young girl of thirteen, who she recognized as Claudia, the young precocious child that had been kidnapped while Captree and she were in New York investigating the serial killer, now known as the Cross Killer. She sat there in her ambivalence wanting to forgive him, but she was conflicted. How do you forgive an adulterer just a short time after he sleeps with you? Her emotions spilled over, and she walked over to Claudia, hugged her and began to cry with Claudia.

"I'm so sorry dear child. Hopefully your dad will pull through."

"Thank you, Detective Saunders. I really appreciate you making the trip up here."

"Don't mention it. I like your dad and I knew you would need support."

They sat together just waiting and not saying a word, when suddenly a groan emanated from the bed. They looked up simultaneously at the face of Captree, when a faint but definitely perceptive movement was felt by Claudia, who was holding his hand. Then another groan and Claudia said, "My God. He moved. He moved. I felt his finger move in my hand." Then another groan was followed by Captree opening his eyes.

"Dad! Dad! It's Claudia."

Saunders walked out to summon the nurse at this development. A few moments passed and the house doctor strolled in to examine the situation. His examination revealed definite movement and arousal from the coma of the past six days.

The attending thoracic surgeon examined Captree next and declared, "I believe this is great progress. He's coming out of the coma, and I think that he may indeed pull through."

Claudia hugged her dad's chest and declared with joy. "Thank God, Thank you, God."

Saunders stared at the awakening Captree and remained perplexed and conflicted but stayed in the room, nonetheless.

My red eye flight to Los Angeles landed at 3am PDT. I rushed back to my dorm room, hurriedly flipped open my laptop to complete the addition that the director had requested. When completed I scanned it and emailed it as a PDF file to the director and then collapsed on my bed completely drained. I slept for approximately three hours when my cell phone buzzing and chiming awoke me with a facetime call, looking at the screen, I was shocked that it was Beth Murray.

"Evan, Are you there?"

"Beth? What is it? You woke me. I'm exhausted."

"I'm sorry but I had to tell you as soon as possible."

"Huh? I hardly know you. What is it?"

"I'm coming to Los Angeles with a friend of mine form Beaumont. You may even know her. Imani Moss. She was a few years ahead of us. Do you remember her?"

"Shit, Beth, I've been up all night on a flight to California and then all morning working on my screenplay and you're fucking playing guessing games with me?"

"Hey. Come on. I'm excited to be coming to LA and seeing you again."

"Okay. What about this Imani? I'm not sure I recall her at all."

"Anyway, she's a Black girl, who I 've known since we were kids. She called me last night and told me this horrible story. Interestingly, it was very similar to my own experience. Her friend Julie Simpson was found in her apartment murdered by a slasher. The entire scenario was reminiscent of Emily. He cut her throat, raped her and left a defining mark on her chest: A Cross. She was completely devastated and needs to get out of Boston, so she's coming to New York and we're going to take a vacation to California. I had to tell you. I wanted her to meet you since we're all old Beaumont alums. Isn't that super?"

"Shit, Beth did you really think that I wanted to spend my time escorting you and this chick so she can assuage her sadness and feelings of loss? Do I seem like a therapist to you? Anyway, I have my own issues to deal with."

Immediately realizing that my attitude, words and voice were angry and acrimonious and possibly suspicious, I retracted, "Hey. I'm so sorry. I'm just irritable and fatigued. Yeah. I'd love to meet you when you get to L.A."

"That's the kid I spoke to on the train. I'll text you with the details when we arrive. I'm really looking forward to seeing sunny SoCal."

"Great. Looking forward to it," I lied, "Bye, Beth, speak to you soon."

I hung up and leaned back on the bed with an uneasy feeling of dread in the pit of my stomach. *This is getting too close to home,* I thought. What if they start adding things up, comparing notes and realize that there is a common element in the Venn diagram of these murders. I felt that depressive force again and shuddered. *My life is closing in on me.*

Agent Joseph Esposito returned from L.A. with the added information of a DNA match of the Colleen Moore murderer and the others that had been analyzed even though her killer had not left the distinctive cross that were carved on the others. Looking at his data sheets he was interrupted by a phone call from an agent in Boston describing the Julie Simpson murder.

"We just finished the analysis of the crime scene here in Boston. I can tell you that the scene is very much like the ones in Los Angeles and in New York. The DNA is still pending, though."

"Did he leave a cross on her chest?"

"Yes. Yes, he did. It is just like he did on the others."

"There was one here in L.A. where he didn't. I wonder what made him change his MO in that one case. There may be a clue there but for the life of me,

I can't understand what it is. Do you think I would be of any use in Boston?"

"I don't believe so," the agent reinforced.

"Okay. Well. Thanks. Let me know if anything else turns up and surely the results of the DNA."

Esposito sat back again examining this overwhelming data: the airlines, and their schedules, the airline tickets, the Amtrak schedules, the credit card information. He couldn't detect a pattern although he firmly believed there had to one there. He needed a good programmer and coder to decipher this mess. *Wasn't there a company that did exactly that,* he wondered? He traced back in his brain to find an answer. He remembered that the LAPD had hired a company to trace criminals, which created a controversy because of the fear of racial profiling. *What the fuck was their name? I think the Feds used them also.* He called the Science and Technology Directorate in Washington, a division of the Department of Homeland Security (DHS) whose vital function was to support the Department of Homeland Security's mission to prevent terrorism by using applied research, scientific based and modern technology. Esposito thought he had read that they hired a company to help in big data analysis to track potential terrorists. He was directed to the Undersecretary's office for Intelligence and Analysis. Although director's position was unfilled, he was able to contact the next in line.

"Hi. My name is Joseph Esposito from the FBI, the Behavioral Analysis Unit. Do you have a minute?'

"I know your division very well. You track serial killers, rapists and violent crimes, right?"

"Yes, we do. Anyway, we're currently investigating a serial killer and rapist in New York, Los Angeles, Boston and Beaumont, Massachusetts."

"Yes. I think I've heard about this case. The Cross Killer, right?"

"Yes. That's the one. Well, this guy seems to be very peripatetic. We have reams of data tracking his various stops, but it is very difficult to coordinate that data into a meaningful pattern. I know you're working with a company involved in big data analysis and tracking terrorists. So, I thought they might be useful in helping to analyze the data we have on this murderer. I heard that they're involved in tracking criminals in Los Angeles so it would seem like a perfect fit."

"That's an interesting thought. I must admit I have never thought about that possibility, but it does make sense especially in a case like yours. You know they have gotten a tremendous amount of criticism for their work because of their involvement with ICE and deportation. They've been vilified even in Los Angeles for their use of racial profiling as one of the methods in their analysis."

"I understand, but if you could just give me some contact information, I'd discuss it with them."

"Sure. The Company is called **Palantir Technologies**® and they have a law enforcement arm so you might try there first."

"Great. Thank so much. That is very helpful. I'll contact them."

Esposito hung up elated; this might be the breakthrough he needs to catch this bastard. He contacted Detective Francis in Los Angeles, who was working on the USC murder and discussed Palantir. Francis knew their function within the LAPD and was able to assist in securing a meeting with the head of the Law Enforcement Division, Josh Forester. A meeting within the week was arranged with Marin, Esposito and the point man from Palantir in LA. Esposito was most encouraged by the details of the technology that Palantir could provide and its ability to track big data. One concern remained, the cost of hiring the company for this work. Esposito knew his budget was limited and that could very well create an obstacle. He would have to clear it with the FBI, but he well knew that the bureaucracy of a federal agency was difficult to navigate. He had to try so he initiated the appropriate contacts. He couldn't do anything else but wait for the inevitable. "Another slaying." This bastard never left a clue as to his intentions or future murders as many other serial killers had. He had to wait anxiously and expectantly for the worse. For an experienced agent in the BAU, this was excruciating. He was always of the mind set to prevent the next murder but today he was in limbo without hope of accomplishing that. He reviewed the data again and again. Why the fuck does he move around so much? What is this SOB's real life like? What are his motives? What is his uniqueness that would expose him? Esposito, who considered himself an expert, remained baffled.

He opened his eyes, looked straight ahead and saw his daughter, consternation but a faint smile on her face and then turned ten degrees leftward and noticed Alexandra Saunders. At first, he didn't recall the circumstances. Claudia saw his eyes shutter and open and came closer to his face.

"Dad, it's Claudia. Do you recognize me?"

"Yes," came the faint whisper.

Saunders remained fixed at the bedside without saying a word but anxious about the development and the possible chance to speak to this man again and explore their relationship further. Over the next two to three days, Ronald Captree awoke further and became more responsive. Since he was still on a ventilator, he was not yet verbal, but Claudia was assured that he would be weaned off over the next twenty-four to thirty-six hours. The doctors and nurses asked her to be patient and suggested that her dad was recuperating, albeit slowly. The thoracic surgeon suggested that it would take some time for him to be her obvious dada. Having to return to her duties, Saunders left Beuamont after the weekend but assured Claudia she would return as soon as she could. She then walked over to Captree bent her head down to his ear and said in a faint tone barely perceptible, "Ronald. I'm glad you're going to be okay. I'll come back as soon as I can, and we'll talk. I did uncover some information that might be helpful to you but first, please get better and well." She waited but there was no response. She hugged Claudia and left the door to head back to New York. Captree closed his eyes and fell asleep.

By my twentieth birthday, I was feeling invincible: I moved out of the dorm to an apartment in Marina del Rey, so called "Mother's Beach", a seaside community known for its eponymous harbor with wide ranging water and boating activities. It's a family and kid friendly man-made beach, which I wanted as part of a non-incriminating pretense. I took a leave of absence from school to concentrate on my writing and the Netflix production. Most of all, my newfound confidence gave me a sense irrepressibility. Within one week of my move to the beach, I received a text from Beth Murray: *Hey, it's Beth. Imani and I are coming to L.A. next week. When do you think we can get together?* I answered with a nebulous response, but I knew that I would have to meet them since I was sure she wouldn't take "no" for an answer no matter how vociferously I declined or objected.

Agent Esposito was in turmoil. He tried every contact possible to gain the necessary funds to secure Palantir Technologies® to help him analyze the voluminous data accumulated concerning the travel history of the Cross Killer but to no avail. He called the IT department of the Bureau to inquire about other possibilities for the Big Data management and learned that Twitter was working on a program that was similar to Palantir's but that it was still in the beta phase. Esposito contacted Twitter's main office and learned that although the program was classified, the Boston office was working on an algorithm to compress Big Data and derive usable information. He was directed to two young engineers leading the effort on the problem, Imani Moss and Julie Simpson. Both were MIT graduates although of different years. Moss was in charge and Simpson had recently come on board. He was delighted and encouraged at this development and contacted the Twitter Human Resource office in Boston, "Hi, my name is Agent Esposito with the FBI Behavioral Analysis Unit. Can you please give me the contact information for Imani Moss? I realize you are not allowed to dispense personal information, but this is official FBI business."

"I can connect you to her office."

"That would be great, thank you."

Imani Moss, sitting in her Pod, answered the call grudgingly, "Yes. How can I help you?"

"Is this Imani Moss? My name is Joseph Esposito. I'm with the FBI, the Behavioral Analysis Unit."

"FBI? What would you want from me, unless this is about Julie Simpson?"

"Well, I did want to speak to both of you."

"You don't know? I'm sorry, you won't be able to speak to Julie. Julie is dead, killed by a maniac."

"Shit That's the Julie Simpson? What a shmuck I am. I didn't put two and two together. Julie Simpson was killed in Boston, of course. She was just murdered by the Cross Killer. She's your associate?"

"She was not only my associate, but she was also a good friend."

"I'm so sorry to hear that. Do you have some time to talk?"

"Honestly, I'm sorry. I really don't. I'm trying to finish up this piece of code before I leave for L.A. on a vacation, tomorrow?"

"Hmm? What if I meet you in L.A.? I was headed there anyway."

"I think I could manage that. By the way, what is this about? I don't know anything about her killing. I told the police everything I know about her: acquaintances, boyfriends, habits, even her exercise schedule and her social habits."

"No. No. I'm sorry. I really don't want to discuss her murder. The FBI and BPD are working on that. I wanted to discuss your work, the algorithm and code you're working on specifically."

"I'm sorry that is confidential and privileged information that is still in development and testing stage and hardly ready for release."

"I understand but if we can discuss it, I'd be most appreciative. It could be very helpful to my investigation."

"I guess there would be no harm in meeting you. I'll be staying at the Westin Bonaventure on S. Figueroa Street, but we'll only be there for a few days. We're heading up to San Francisco after that."

"No problem. When are you arriving?"

"My friend and I are taking the red eye tonight."

Intrigued by this conversation, Imani Moss perceived she might have a role in solving her friend Julie's murder, but fully realizing that her role could very limited if they need the Big Data algorithm she was working on.

"Great. I'll see you at the Westin tomorrow evening. Thank you."

Encouraged by this interesting development, he thought that this could be the breakthrough he was searching for since Moss had a very good reason and be very interested in helping him, since it was her friend, Julie Simpson, who was the victim in Boston.

Esposito asked his assistant to book the first flight out of Ronald Reagan the following day. He called McMaster and asked him to pick him up at LAX the following day explaining the reason for returning to Los Angeles. McMaster was surprised that Esposito was coming back to L.A. but hearing his explanation and the possible use and analysis of the data invigorated him at the prospect of this avenue of the investigation.

Beth Murray and Imani Moss reached their tenth-floor room at 2am and went right to sleep.

252 PHILIP SCHULMAN, MD

The next morning, they had breakfast in the hotel café of scrambled eggs, fruit and coffee for Beth and yogurt with fruit and expresso for Imani. They spent the rest of the day at poolside. Beth tried calling me at noon, but I didn't answer. She tried again at 1pm and then again at 2pm. By 3pm, I was exasperated by her consistency and finally answered.

"Hello. This is Evan Dicks. How can I help you?" I answered mysteriously knowingly undoubtedly that it was Beth who was calling.

"What the fuck is this formality. You know fully who it is."

"Ah yes, Beth. Welcome to L.A. How are you?"

"I'm fine. How are you? How is the show going?"

"I'm good, Beth. The show is going great, and my new work is coming along, also I suppose you called because you'd like to get together."

"You sound skeptical. It's really okay if you don't want to. It's not imperative at all if you're too busy. I'm here with a friend and we'll be leaving for San Francisco in two days. So, it's up to you."

"Hey, can't you take a little sarcasm. Where's that Beaumont sense of humor. Come on. Of, course, I want to meet. Where are you staying? Better yet why don't you and your friend come to the beach. I live in an apartment at Marina del Rey, which is very close to Venice Beach. What did you say your friend's name was again?"

"I told you Imani Mass. She's a Beaumont graduate. I'm not sure she wants to sit and discuss old

Beaumont times. She's still not over the gruesome killing of her friend Julie Simpson and is having a terrible time of it. But I will ask her. Give me your address. We rented a car so we can drive over."

"Great. Looking forward to it."

The mention of Julie sent a tremor through my being. *How would I react to her friend being here and discussing the murder of Julie Simpson, my latest victim? And then how would she react to meeting someone from Beaumont, who knew her, and who knew Emily O'Connor? The strangeness of these coincidences was beyond comprehension and frightening to me to say the least.*

Looking around the vast extravagant lobby of the Westin, Joseph Esposito was trying to organize his thoughts as to the best approach with this young, obviously brilliant engineer to convince her to use the nascent version of her algorithm to locate a pattern for the movement of this maniacal serial killer. When she exited the elevator, he easily recognized the tall black female with a stylish cut Afro from her description. He arose walked toward her and acknowledging her.

"Hi, Agent Joseph Esposito," he said revealing his FBI credential.

"It's nice to meet you. I'm Imani Moss."

"I gathered. Would you like to go to the café? Have you eaten yet?"

They entered the tile floored café and were shown a private side booth toward the back of tiled walled restaurant. While she read the menu he asked, "What would you like? It's on the United States government."

"Just coffee, thanks."

"Cup of coffee for the lady and I'll have a hamburger and coke," he said to the waitress. "I'm starving. I haven't eaten since my early morning flight," he added speaking to Imani.

"So, let me start at the beginning. I've been investigating this case since the perpetrator killed a young journalist in Los Angeles. He also killed a woman in Beaumont, Massachusetts, two women in New York, a woman on the Northeast corridor Amtrak on the way to New York and a woman in Boston."

He searched her face for a reaction and her expression revealed her shock and amazement. He knew this disclosure was a surprise to her. He knew she had firsthand knowledge of the Julie Simpson murder, but now the revelation of multiple similar murders seemed to shock, amaze and perplex her.

"Well, anyway we have extensive data on his travel itinerary, including tickets, credit card information, airline flights and schedules and Amtrak schedules between Boston, New York and Los Angeles. I was hoping to collate this Big Data into a cogent form to easily track individuals within this morass. I wanted to hire Palantir Tech®, but unfortunately the Feds wouldn't or couldn't generate the funds. The IT guy at the agency mentioned that he heard Twitter was working on similar technology. Voila! Imani Moss. To top that off, you happen to be a good friend of one of the victims and thus, have extra motivation."

"I appreciate what you're saying but our code and algorithms are still in Beta testing and far from ready for prime time."

"I understand, I'm only asking to run our data through your program and see if it leads anywhere. If we could just single out a handful of names with a comparable travel schedule, it would be very helpful in our search for this psycho. Plus, as a sidelight, it could help validate your program."

"I'm sorry, I'll have to clear this with our Legal Department, Content Department and our COO." "Yes, that's understood, but if you could expedite those approvals, I would really appreciate it."

"Okay, I'll make the necessary calls as soon as I can. You do know that I'm on vacation here in California?"

"Oh yes! Have a nice trip to San Francisco."

Moss looked at him quizzically and thought, How *the fuck did he know we were headed to San Francisco. I guess that's why he's the FBI.* "Yeah, thanks. I'll call you when I know anything," she said taking his card. She left the restaurant leaving her cup of coffee only half finished as he ate his hamburger. She took the elevator back up to the tenth floor, knocked the door of 1008 and waited for a response.

After a minute, having not taken her key, she went back to the front desk identified herself and told them she had left her key in her room and asked for a spare key. Entering the room, she found her phone and called Beth.

"Hey, where are you. I'm famished and wanted to do something today and then go to dinner?"

"I'm so sorry, babe. I called Evan Dicks and he suggested I come out to the beach to his new apartment."

"What the fuck? I thought we were going to see him together."

"I mentioned you to him and he didn't remember you so I thought that it might be best to just see him by myself tonight, and then we'll drive up toward San Francisco tomorrow, Okay?"

"I guess, but it would have been nice to rehash old Beaumont times. By the way, how is he? I heard his parents were in a brutal suicide murder and they were both killed."

"Yeah, his father found his mother in bed with Capt. Captree, lost it and shot them both, killing his mother and then shot himself."

"Wow, Gruesome. How is Evan?"

"Here's the phone. Ask him yourself."

"Hello, Imani. Is that you?"

"Yeah. How are you?"

"I'm hanging in, thanks. Sorry you couldn't make it to the beach, but anyway good hearing your voice and thanks for your concern, bye."

"Bye, Evan, see ya."

"I'm, I'll probably be here another couple of hours and then come back to the hotel. Have a good dinner."

Thanks, see ya later." Moss hung up the phone, turned on the T.V in the room staring at it in disappointment. After watching an inane movie, she walked out of the room and headed back to the café for dinner.

Beth turned to me and suggested we take a walk on the beach. I related that the Marina only has a man-made beach without much of a beach head. I suggested we should go to Venice, which was only a mile away. She was delighted having heard many stories about the craziness of Venice beach: people watching on the promenade, seeing the bodybuilders at Muscle Beach, watching the fantastic skateboarders at Skate Park, gawking at the online skaters occasionally performing with either a guitar or mouth harp, the marijuana dispensaries and the hordes of people who frequented them and of course, the wonderful Mexican food. Reaching the beach in less than fifteen minutes, Beth parked in an outdoor lot, and we strolled toward the surf. We stopped at a small taqueria and had tacos and fajitas with Dos Exes. After a pleasant conversation for an hour, we arose as I paid the check. We then headed for the promenade. We walked hand in hand through the extremely crowded walkway, stopped at a railing and turned to look at the surf staring out at the rolling waves of the Pacific.

"You know, Evan. I think my friends and I really blew it. You are really nice and nothing we perceived you to be, but yet we always thought you were such a nerd. The kids bullied you, didn't they?"

"No, no. Not the girls. They really didn't. They just ignored me, but those jocks, they were the worst.

I guess they didn't appreciate literature, art and culture, but then again, I didn't appreciate football. I guess, most of the girls weren't very nice, either. I was really hurt and angered by your general attitude."

"That's why I just revealed my newfound appreciation for your talent, and I discovered that you're really cool. Hey, Evan, didn't you come to Emily's graduation party?"

"Yes, yes I did, but I didn't stay too long."

"Yeah, I know. Emily told me."

Diffidently I asked, "What else did she say?"

"Oh, not much, but she did mention that she talked to you, and you seemed to be very nice, and she thought about possibly asking you out."

"Asking me out? Do girls really do that?"

"Not most, but Emily did all the time. Did she ever follow through with that?"

"Uh, no. She never asked me out."

"You seemed to hesitate. Did you ever meet her after the party?"

"No. Why are you asking?"

"Well, as you know Emily was like a tiger. When she wanted something, she wholeheartedly went after it. Emily was never one to take no for an answer or to not follow up on her wishes or desires, so I was only asking."

"No, we never met. We never went out," I replied feeling uneasy about this conversation and quite uncomfortable and realizing my fears in meeting Beth, "But the fact that you mentioned that exasperates me even further. Why the fuck do I need to hear this now after you and your friends treated me like a leper for four years?"

"Evan, I'm sorry for even discussing this. You're absolutely right; it is uncalled for and unfair. I'm really sorry, Evan. Please, forgive me."

I didn't respond. I grabbed her hand and said, "Come, Let's go. It's getting late."

She looked at me quizzically and stated, "Really? I have time. I'm really having a nice time and I love the beach."

"I don't think so. We have to leave now!"

She looked at me shockingly but reluctantly followed my lead as we walked to her car. We drove a short distance and at a red light, I asked her to turn into a dark secluded area behind the marina. She seemed startled by this request but followed my instruction unenthusiastically.

"Why, what is it?" In the middle of the street, I asked her to stop the car at a curb. When at a standstill, I turned to her, grabbed her chin forcefully and kissed her pushing my tongue into her mouth. Predictably, she returned my kiss with a strong hug and sigh. She stroked my face as I caressed her breast. Her sigh turned into a groan, and I slowly moved my hand down her shorts. As her passion rose, I removed my knife and slashed her throat, her face and her chest. The terror in her face again brought me to the brink and I continued slashing finally feeling that release. I carved the cross on her chest and sat still for a few moments, contemplating my action.

Oh my God. What have I done? Her friend Imani knows we're together. I have just set myself up to be suspect number one. But I understood. There is a driving force in my psyche that propels these acts. Even if I was rational, which I'm not, and tried to understand and try to stop, I couldn't. That force is too powerful. And this fucking slut with her friends, who tormented my life for years, deserved it, just as her buddy, Emily, did.

I composed myself, thought about what I needed to do now and proceeded to drive her car towards L.A.I parked off Sunset near a near a rock club, grabbed her phone and texted Imani Moss:

Hey, I just left Evan's place and decided to stop at a rock club on Sunset for some music and a comedown. Evan and I had a nice time, but he got very indignant and depressed when we talked about his time at Beaumont High. The beach was beautiful and overall had some laughs. I think that I want to see him again. He's an entirely different person than the dork I knew in high school. See ya.

Perfect, I thought. I cleaned off the phone, left the keys in the car and walked away, carefully checking for possible witnesses, which thankfully I didn't see. I ran to Sunset and took a bus back to the Marina. I entered the apartment, grabbed a beer and sat at my laptop to continue writing the new book I was working on. I worked on it until 3am and closed the laptop and slowly walked into the bedroom. I reclined on the bed and closed my eyes, but my mind raced, and sleep was futile. I thought about Beth, the shock and terror etched in her face and eyes and my response to it. I slowly felt the tension leave my being and finally fell asleep.

Alexandra noticed that Captree wanted to say something, so she slowly bent her ear to his mouth, "Alex, please forgive me. I was telling Sarah Dicks that it's over. We didn't do anything. You have to believe me," he whispered.

"You just rest. We have plenty of time to discuss this. You just get well. Claudia needs you.

"Thanks," she barely perceptibly heard him say and he closed his eyes. Unfortunately, she never got the chance to discuss the findings regarding the Amtrak data that Martin and she had uncovered. She hugged Claudia and left for New York again on the evening shuttle.

Chapter 21

The Netflix production of "Deadly Motivations" was proceeding seamlessly. The director was mostly pleased with my work, which made me feel quite assured. The estimate was for broadcast the following year, which encouraged me. Watching the rehearsals and the actual filming was the highlight of my dark days. I thought about Maria, but I never called her. When not in the studio, I continued to write. I was working on a novel and a nonfiction crime piece. I never watched the nightly news broadcasts or read a newspaper, so I had no idea how the investigation into killings was proceeding, nor did I really care. I was resigned to the inevitable but had no power to prevent it or to stop my killing.

Following the death of Beth Murray and need for resolution, Imani Moss was able to secure the approval of the legal department the COO, and content department to help the FBI investigation using the New Big Data algorithm at Twitter®. Moss, obtaining a leave of absence from her supervisor and traveling to Virginia, she met Agent Esposito at the Behavioral Analysis Unit in Quantico. As soon as she walked into the door, she saw Esposito, who gave her the data he had collected and directed her to a small cubicle workstation. She was issued a temporary ID and an FBI laptop with modifications and access to only the data concerning the Cross Killer case. Imani had experienced intense anger, depression and vulnerability at having two of her friends murdered in a short interval and obviously by the same person as the DNA of the perpetrator matched. Her sense of helplessness was assuaged somewhat by this assignment. Her work also alleviated the lugubriousness at the loss of Beth and Julie. Her conversations with Esposito were unrevealing as to his thought processes. Yet she couldn't help but think that Beth had met Evan Dicks the night before her murder and thus, he had to be a prime suspect. She told Esposito the same, but he seemed to dismiss Dicks as a suspect in that it appeared that Beth had picked someone up at the club and he was the one that killed her. Imani was baffled that he didn't at least deem it necessary to question Dicks. She fervently hoped the travel data would reveal Evan Dicks' movements to at least question him and obtain a DNA sample.

But Esposito was only being coy; he had already set up surveillance of Dicks in order to try to obtain a serendipitous DNA sample. Carefully awaiting the data breakdown, Esposito receive a message from Sgt. Martin in Beaumont.

"Is this Agent Joseph Esposito?" asked Martin.

"Yes, it is. How can I help you?"

"I'm Sgt. Martin. I work with Capt. Captree. You may very well know that we've been working with Det. Alexandra Saunders form the NYPD regarding the Cross Killer."

"Yes. Captree had mentioned that she was working on the Amtrak incident. He had mentioned that she had visited Beaumont a few times also."

"Well, the truth is she's been here more often recently to visit Ronald."

"Why would she visit him? Do they have something going?"

"I think they do, but the reason she's been up here so frequently is that Captree is in the hospital. He was shot by a jealous husband, who found him in bed with his wife."

"Sorry, I'm not interested in the Peyton Place scenario of Beaumont. But what can I help you with? Why the call?"

"Well, it turns out Saunders discovered a name that consistently came up in the Amtrak ticketing and scheduling data?"

"Yes? I'm listening."

Imani sat at her cubicle working feverishly with data. There were multiple names that that were possibilities including Evan Dicks, but the novelty of the program reflected the many inaccuracies and impreciseness of the system that needed to be corrected before a valid result could be assured. Nevertheless, she noted some possibilities and interestingly enough, the name, Evan Dicks was prominent. The same guy Beth had visited and a Beaumont graduate. She closed the program, felt comfort and elation at her discovery and walked over to Esposito excitedly. Unfortunately, he had left for the day. She checked her watch and noted that it was past midnight, and no one was still at the Bureau. She left the building headed for her nearby hotel and waited for the following day.

Arriving the next day, Esposito appeared in excellent spirits. He acknowledged all his office workers, made his own cup of coffee and asked anyone nearby, "So how is everyone this morning? Isn't it absolutely a wonderful day?"

"What's gotten into you today?"

"What have you been smoking or better yet taking?"

"Nothing at all. Just feeling real good as I believe we're close to cracking the Cross Killer mystery."

"Really?"

"Yeah, I'm still waiting for a bit more information. I do have some suspects and I'm trying to get DNA samples to compare to those that we already have."

"Why not ask the suspects, directly."

"They can refuse, and we need a court order so it would be great if we could obtain one furtively."

As he was completing the explanation, Imani Moss entered his office sat at the desk and waited for his acknowledgement.

He told his assistant to please step out and asked Imani directly, "So you had about twelve hours with this data, right? What did you find?"

"Yes, I worked all day yesterday and didn't leave this place until after midnight. Now you have to remember that we're still in the early stage of development of this program and I'm sure it's inexact and unfocussed, but anyway I do have some results that might be helpful to you."

"That's what I wanted to hear. When I awoke this morning that is exactly what I was hoping for and excited about. Okay, what have you got?"

Moss said in matter-of-fact terms, "There are a number of names that are possibilities and repeatedly match. Thus, I think you'll need to follow the lead on all of them."

"I understand. But tell me is Evan Dicks on the list?"

I felt an ominous dread. There seemed to be someone following me in a government issued car. Everywhere I went I, noticed the same car and the same official looking characters. I thought that that I'm under surveillance and would need to be especially careful about everything I touch. I would have to be fastidious about my garbage, my apartment, my mail and my surroundings. I realized it would be difficult not to eventually err, but I knew that I desperately needed to try. The feeling of being close to capture increased my obvious depression. But I could only blame myself. I was reckless and careless. I left myself open to discovery, especially with the murder of Beth Murray. But what could I do? I already knew that the overpowering feeling of needing to accomplish the objective was impossible to inhibit or curb. So, the result had to be what I was experiencing. As I left my apartment, I noticed the Uber that I had called. I gave the driver the address of the studio producing my script. As we drove, I kept looking out the back window and that damn car, a late mode Ford was always right behind us. There was no pretense of a clandestine operation. It was if they wanted me to know that they were there and closing in. I reached the studio. Entering the studio, I was greeted by the director.

"Evan. Hey how goes? I have to admit the show is coming along great and your changes and additions are spot on. I am very surprised by your efficiency and talent for such a very young author and playwright."

"Thanks. That means a lot to me.

The scene they were filming was of a young recently recruited terrorist hiding in Brazil and realizing that his capture was imminent. I realized it almost paralleled by own situation which seemed ironic. I watched the filming, which gratified me, but was poignant realizing that I was near the denouement. I continued to watch my words come to life and thought that at least I would have a legacy even though remembered as a psychopathic killer. I closed my eyes and felt a deep sadness, almost as if I was repenting. I knew that this was hardly possible. I had to leave the studio as the feelings overwhelmed me and walked out. I walked around the environs of the studio and noticed the two feds surveilling me. Composed, I walked back in, sat at the writer's seat and continued to observe, waiting for the inevitable. But they never approached me or talked to me. They were just observing me carefully, meticulously and intently. How could I not stumble at some point?

The day's shooting finished at nightfall. I walked out, found the Uber I had called waiting and we drove back to the beach. Again, I observed the intense surveillance of my every move.

Chapter 22

When I returned to the apartment, I decided that I needed to get away from this intense scene. I called the director of the production. Ana Janssen, to let her know that I needed a break and that I'd be working remotely from Las Vegas. I told her that I would be heading there for a few days of relaxation and some fun. She seemed disappointed in this as she needed me to be present, but she agreed to cooperate with my request understanding the pressure that I must have been under given my age and inexperience. The production had to move forward to meet the deadlines set by Netflix and couldn't possibly halt at this point. They were anxious to showcase the production for possible forthcoming festivals or advertisers during the new season conventions.

I logged onto the website for the Circa Hotel and Casino, the newest incarnation of Las Vegas glitz, but located on Fremont Street not on the Strip. The five-hundred-foot-high hotel is known for the Stadium Swim with three pools all overlooked by a forty-foot high-definition TV screen and being the tallest Hotel/Casino north of the Strip. What enticed me was the multi-level swimming pool with cabanas and day beds and the idea of empty relaxation free of stress, surveillance and my secret life. I thought if I'm going to Vegas to unwind, this would be the perfect venue; it was away from the hustle of the gambling scene although a three-story casino was part of the complex. While booking a room, I also rented a car to drive there. I was a bit ambivalent about gambling, but I did have a fake ID I could use if necessary for bars, strip clubs and the casino.

I awoke the next morning at 7am, made coffee and had cereal for breakfast and waited for my car, which was to be delivered to my home at 9am. The car was a late model Toyota Prius. The drive to Las Vegas approximately two hundred and seventy miles away was pleasant. I took the scenic route out of LA onto CA-2 and followed that through the perimeter of the Mojave National Preserve on I-15-N into Las Vegas. Happiness, relief and a sense of security marked my psyche as I registered at the front desk. I entered my room on the twenty-eighth floor, looked out at the spectacular view of the entire Las Vegas strip, surrounding the desert amid a cloudless blue sky. I slowly undressed put on my Patagonia swim trunks and went down to the third story pool. I picked out a chaise facing the big screen TV and reclined with a towel over my head and lemonade at my side. I must have fallen asleep, for the next thing I remembered was a feeling of cold drops of water on my chest then my face. I opened my eyes and looked up at a smiling, pretty brunette with blue eyes and a tan.

"Hey, wake up it's getting late."

"Late for what? I don't have any appointments."

"Late to take me to dinner," she laughed.

"Who said I was taking you to dinner? I don't know who the hell you are."

"All you have to do is ask."

"Okay, who are you?"

"My name is Holly. I'm staying here at the hotel. But most importantly, I don't have dinner plans."

"That's interesting. Neither do I, but then again, I ask; who said I wanted to take you dinner?"

Sitting down on the chaise next to me she, authoritatively, said, "Let's discuss it then." I looked at her, my curiosity piqued and said, "Okay, let's talk."

She was garrulous and continued to talk for the next ten minutes without interruption. She stated she was from the Midwest, was in Vegas with a friend who had met a stranger at a bar last night and has not answered her texts or phone since.

"I guess you'll be travelling back to the Midwest alone then."

"I don't think so. I think you'll be coming with me," she laughed.

"You're quite assertive, aren't you? How do you know I'm not here with someone and you're only wasting your time?"

"Well, I took the chance."

I looked at her again and was quite fascinated by this self-confident, loquacious, young woman and suggested that I'd love to shower and change first and then meet at Saginaw's Deli on the first casino floor of the hotel. She happily agreed and we set the time to meet for 7pm. Arising from the lounge, I put a towel around my waist and said, "Great, see you." I waved to her as I walked to the elevator and rode up to my room. I showered, shaved, and put on musk cologne, slim fitting Levi's jeans and a long-sleeved collarless tee shirt. Walking into the deli, I was struck by this classic New York Jewish Deli smell of pickles and cured meats. I searched the booths but could not spot her, so I requested a table and was led to a corner booth in the back. At 7:15, Holly, dressed in a mini dress with a Gucci bag on her shoulder, walked in. Her hair was loose and flowing to her shoulders. She strolled over to my booth and said, "Hey, stranger, fancy meeting you here."

"I don't think so. Did your friend ever get in touch with you again?"

"Oh, yeah. She'll be occupied with that guy until we leave for home, she said. So, I'm all yours."

I laughed, again impressed by her insolence and suggested we order. She ordered the Reuben with a

Diet Coke and I got Pastrami on rye with mustard with a Corona, making use of my fake ID. We finished dinner in about one and a half hours. Our conversation was lively and fun. She had a great sense of humor and was very friendly, but there was something about this entire scenario that bothered me. I didn't understand her motives or her intent. Why would this cute young woman be interested in me? I was her junior by at least five years. Her interest in my writing might have been an explanation. I did mention my book and its acceptance by Netflix. But still why be interested in hanging with me, a comparatively naïve and inexperienced kid. Surprisingly as we walked out of Saginaw's, she said, "Let's go up to my room for a nightcap."

It all became obvious when I hesitated and she said, "For one hundred, I'll give you the best blow job you ever had."

"I am totally disappointed. I really thought you were into me and you're a fucking hooker. Shit that is a bunch of crap." I started walking away when she followed me, tapped me on the shoulder and proclaimed, "Hey. Don't get mad. I am into you and do think you're fun, but I have to survive.in this crazy fucked up world."

"Get a fucking real job, you slut."

"Come on. Make it seventy-five."

"Do you really have a room because I am definitely not taking you up to mine?"

"Yeah, I have a room and we can spend as long as you like for a price, of course."

"Okay, Let's go, but just the blow job."

"Follow me. It's on the fifteenth floor."

"What room. I don't want to be seen going up to hotel room with a fucking hooker."

"Room 1511. I'll go up first. Meet me there."

I watched the elevator car door close after she left and waited for the next open elevator car door. I remained there, outside the restaurant, debating whether to follow her up. It could be dangerous and hardly worth the cash, but my mind told me otherwise. When I perceived that "feeling", that uncontrollable "urge", I knew that I had to teach this slut a lesson. I waited at that spot frozen for a few moments when my psyche assumed control over my actions. I followed her up to the fifteenth floor with an ambivalent sense of excitement and dread, overwhelming compulsion and anxiety, elation and sorrow. My entire psychological mindset revealed itself in those few moments.

I knocked on the door and "Holly" answered it wearing a skimpy nightie without underwear. She put her arms around me, gave me a hug and whispered to lie on the bed. She stood over me at the edge of the bed, dropped her nightshirt and stared into my face, "Nice huh?"

"Yes," I moaned, "very nice."

She bent down undid my jeans and bent to kiss my penis. I suddenly opened the switch blade in my hand and slashed the back of her neck. She bent her head back reflexively and screamed, "Oh!" I slashed her again along the side of her neck. Looking into her eyes, I saw the terror, shock, and surprise and yelled at her, "You fucking slut. How does that feel?" I slashed her again on her face, chest and abdomen. I then carved the cross on her chest. While carving the cross on her breast, I felt the release that I so needed. I then sensed the energy leave my being and I slumped to the floor. Overwhelming depression overtook my mind, and I couldn't move for a few moments. When I was rejuvenated, I arose, washed off, put on my shirt and jeans and left the room carefully observing for interlopers.

I rode the elevator down to the second-floor casino and stopped at the twenty-five-dollar crap table. I revealed my fake ID, which was accepted ordered chips for two hundred and fifty dollars in twenty-five-dollar denominations and placed twenty-five dollars on the pass line. The shooter threw an eight and I backed the first bet with odds and placed another twenty-five dollars on the come line. The shooter threw a four. I placed a second bet on the come line and backed the first come bet with odds. The shooter then threw a seven and I crapped out losing one hundred and fifty dollars with one roll of the dice, but I was hardly disappointed. The gambling loss allowed me to feel some retribution for my acts. I understand one hundred fifty dollars hardly constitutes justice for all of my murders, but then again, my twisted mind perceived it as such.

I asked the cocktail waitress for a single malt scotch, finished it and stepped away from the craps table heading for my room. I thought my Las Vegas adventure was now over and that I would leave the following morning.

Detective Henry Rogers of the Las Vegas Police Department Homicide division strode into the posh Circa Hotel room to a grisly scene of mayhem. The victim was sprawled on the bed covered in blood. There was blood on the floor and in addition, it had spurted onto the walls. The CSI was there, as was the medical examiner. "Holly," whose real name was Madeline Foster, was indeed from the Midwest brought to Las Vegas by a notorious talent agency, CreateStar Agency, in the pretense of promoting her for a lead role as a singer and dancer in the major production show at Mandalay Bay. The agency was headed by one Tommy Bentorini, who was under investigation for sex trafficking and prostitution by The LVPD Vice Division. Thus far, he had eluded indictment, but this case may be the clincher. Interviewing the hotel staff at the front desk and the lobby, Rogers learned that "Holly" had dinner with a young man at Saginaw's. Before asking the waitress to come to the station after she completed her rotation to meet him downtown, he went to the kitchen staff and cashier to locate dirty plates, glasses, silver ware and any money for possible DNA sampling. Unfortunately, no one could be sure which utensils or cash was from the booth they sat at.

"Thanks for coming down to the station. I though best we speak in private," Rogers said to the pretty waitress. Who had taken a cab to the station for the hotel?

"Sure," she said. "Wow I was shocked when I heard that the pretty young lady was killed. I heard it was a horrific scene."

"Yeah, it was pretty gruesome. We think she was killed by a known serial killer known as, the Cross Killer. Have you heard of him?"

"I did read in the papers about some Los Angeles murders, but I don't really know much else."

"Well, he's killed a number of young women in LA, New York and Massachusetts, but I believe we're getting close to finding out who he is."

"How can I help?" she asked.

Rogers produced a fax photo that he had received form Esposito of the FBI of a prime suspect and showed it to the cooperative waitress, "Is this the man she had dinner with?"

She inspected the photo carefully and although the photograph was a few years old, she said, "That's him alright. He's a bit older and his hair is longer, and he looks much better now, more confident and self-assured, but no doubt, that's him."

"Is there anything else you can tell me? Did they leave together? Did they pay with a credit card? Did they argue at all?"

"They seemed very cozy and friendly. He paid with cash, and they left together heading for the casino." You didn't see them enter an elevator, did you?"

"No, no I didn't."

"Okay. You've been very helpful. Here is my card if anything else comes to mind. Thanks again for coming down."

Rogers also interviewed the cashier, the hostess and the manager, who all confirmed that the photograph was definitely the person "Holly" was with. He called Esposito as soon as he completed the interview with the good news.

"Hey Agent Esposito, this is Henry Rogers of Las Vegas homicide."

"Yes," replied the FBI agent anxiously and excitedly.

"Well, I think you have your man. All the parties at Saginaw's confirmed that the victim had dinner with the suspect you identified. By the way, the prostitute he had dinner with worked at the Mandalay Bay big production show and was represented by the CreateStar Talent Agency, which we think may be a front for a sex trafficking ring so we may be able to solve two cold crimes with this one case. That would be gravy on the mashed potatoes, eh?"

"Yeah, yeah. Well thanks you very much for calling. I'll keep in touch."

Esposito leaned back in his chair with an evident smile of contentment on his face. He thought of the facts as he saw them and tried to synthesize the conclusion. And recount the obvious details: Evan

Dicks, an insular, loner raised by a brutal father and possibly abusive adulterous mother goes on a killing spree for questionable revenge, retribution, or punishment. His father in an act of rage at discovering his unfaithful wife with a police captain shoots them both killing his wife and then himself. Meanwhile multiple innocent young women are destroyed in a most hideous manner. He had previously investigated similar stories so many times, but the uniqueness of this case stood out, was the age of the perpetrator and the social standing of the family. He called the LA office and spoke to McMaster.

"I think we have our guy," he exclaimed. "Time to bring him in."

McMaster replied, "We haven't gotten a DNA sample yet. Do you want to wait to see if we get a sample first?"

"I'm concerned that he could kill again, so I think we should locate him and bring him in now. He just killed someone in Vegas." We do have photograph identification that he was with the victim in Las Vegas hours before she was killed so I think that's enough to bring him in and even possibly hold him. Esposito was thinking of Imani's data. Her analysis revealed only one name that could have accomplished the travel itinerary of the suspected killer. That name was Evan Dicks. He left Beaumont for New York during the summer. Returned to Beaumont for Thanksgiving weekend and then left again on an Amtrak commuter to New York, the exact train, where the murder victim was discovered at the Newark Airport station. The plane tickets to Los Angeles were consistent with his movement to Los Angeles. This confluence of data coupled with that of the New York detective Saunders, who had articulated a similar schedule for the suspect, to Sgt. Martin, of the Beaumont sheriff's office revealed only one name. That name was Evan Dicks. Thus, he felt confident that the DNA samples would surely match, and Dicks was the offender.

"Okay, you're the boss."

"Thanks."

I spoke to the director and let her know I was returning to Los Angeles and would be back the next day. I asked about the production, and she sounded elated at its progress. This somewhat comforted me and inspired me. I packed my bags, and electronically checked out. I turned the lights off, turned on the TV and opened my laptop to my most recent written thoughts. I made a few corrections and additions, closed the computer, turned off the lights and left the room carefully observing for any persons and when all was clear, I sneaked down the stairs, I entered the parking lot, found the rented Prius, pushed the start button and turned left out of the lot. I turned right onto Fremont, reached Las Vegas Blvd without noticing anyone following me. I turned right onto Las Vegas Blvd and sped toward I-15 and Los Angeles. I sighed in relief at safely having left and carefully went over in mind my next steps. I knew that probably I would somehow have to sneak into my apartment as the four-hour trip would allow sufficient time for the LA authorities to be waiting for me. I thought about another option, which would be to check into a hotel along the route and complete the final chapter. I found a non-descript motel along the route, checked in under an alias and opened the door to a sparse appearing room with a modest thirty-two-inch flat screen TV, a king size bed and a small dresser. I leaned back on the bed and contemplated my next move. I prepared everything for the denouement, the eventual final chapter. I took out my laptop, opened the word document to my new book. I looked at the page, contemplated and reviewed my words and knew instinctively how I would end it.

Chapter 23

Sitting in my darkened room and watching the nighttime news, I realized my apprehension was imminent, but I had evaded capture for at least a few hours as the LVPD had to trace my steps out of the Circa Hotel and would not know the direction I had headed. The Las Vegas Police Department had announced that there was an All-Points Bulletin for the suspected killer of a Las Vegas prostitute. My name biography, and picture were displayed with the headline:

The suspect in the Las Vegas Circa murder and presumed serial killer: The so-called Cross Killer is one Evan Dicks. He is presumed dangerous. Any information please call 1-800-555-0177.

The news broad caster continued:

The Circa Hotel and Casino was the scene of a horrific murder last night. A young woman, an alleged prostitute was discovered murdered by a slasher execution. The killer is suspected to be this man (revealing my photograph): He has committed murders in Massachusetts, New York, Los Angeles, Boston and now Las Vegas. He is a nineteen-year-old man, medium height with longish, brown hair and wears wire-rimmed glasses. Displaying my picture, the reporter continued, he has yet to be apprehended. He goes by the name of Evan Dicks and is considered extremely dangerous. The Las Vega Police Department tells us that he's probably still in Las Vegas and they are creating a net around the city and thus, are hopeful of arresting him very soon.

Panicked but feeling lucky that I had already left the city, I turned off the TV and decided there would be no time for anything further in my life, so I prepared for the inevitable. First, I would call my brother and then I would call Maria and then…

"Hello, Jimmy, is that you?" I asked.

"Evan where are you, what's going on? I saw your picture on TV as the Cross Killer. Evan is that really you? I'm scared. Please tell me it's not. That it's a mistake and they're talking about someone else," he cried.

"I'm sorry Jimmie. Goodbye," I sighed and hung up.

With much trepidation and remorse, I dialed Maria.

"Maria, it's Evan."

"Evan? Is that really you?"

"Yes. Maria. It is. I'm in deep shit. I'm in trouble for doing some very awful things."

"Where are you? Is there anything I can help you with?"

"I'm sorry I can't tell you. I'm in hiding, but I think I'm about to be arrested."

"Arrested? What the hell did you do?"

"Are you telling me you haven't heard?"

"Heard what?"

"There is a nationwide manhunt for the Cross Killer. Maria, I'm the Cross Killer."

She exclaimed incredulously with evident and expectant anger, "What? The Cross Killer? You?"

"Yes. I've killed a number of women and I'm about to be apprehended, but I needed to talk to you first and ask your forgiveness for making a mess of our relationship, for dragging you into my life and for lying to you. You're the best connection I've ever had with another human being. Our relationship comforted my fractured psyche and provided me reassurance, support and peace, but I fucking ruined it all. I'm not sure how strongly you felt about me, but I know that I should have been more appreciative of your encouragement and treated you with more honesty. For that, I had to call you and tell you."

She screamed back, "Evan, what the fuck are you saying? You're telling me the boy I fucked and loved and even brought home to my parents is a fucking serial killer, a psychopath? Evan, you're crazy. I do care about you, but this is insane. I don't understand what you're talking about or any of this shit."

"Yes, Maria, I am. You can turn on the Evening News and confirm what I am saying. So now Maria I have to accomplish one more thing. I need to resolve the conflicts and insanity you just spoke about and there's only way to do that."

"Evan! What the hell are you going to do?"

"Maria. I'm so, so sorry."

I know she heard the pain in my voice, but I couldn't exactly tell her my intentions, so I completed the conversation and again said, "Please forgive me."

"Evan. No, please don't hang up. You're going to hurt yourself, aren't you? Please, Evan, don't do it. Please."

I heard the last pleading tone but did not respond to it or acknowledge it and hung up.

Maria believing that Evan Dicks was about to commit suicide dialed the Las Vegas Police Department and was able to get through to the Downtown Homicide Division and she related her conversation with Evan Dicks.

"Las Vegas Downtown. How can I help you?"

"Hello, my name is Maria Lopez. I'm a friend of Evan Dicks and just got off the phone with him."

"Evan Dicks? The Evan Dicks. You know there is an APB out on him for murder? He might be the Cross Killer."

"Yes, I know. He told me. Anyway, he sounded like he was about to commit suicide. He didn't tell me where he was, but you have to find him. He's severely depressed and I'm sure he's going to kill himself."

"It looks like he left Vegas since we checked his room and he had checked out and left. We have notified the LAPD that he might be returning to his residence in LA. We are also contacting all the hotels and motels for here to LA and also all the north, east and south routes. He couldn't have gotten far, and his picture is plastered all over the media. We'll find him. Thanks for calling us."

"Thank you. Please hurry," Maria cried.

The clerk at the motel, for want of anything else to do on a secluded highway in the middle of the night, was transfixed by the small TV in the lobby, when the news bulletin that Evan had seen came on: The suspect in the Las Vegas Circa murder and presumed serial killer: The so-called Cross Killer is one Evan Dicks. He is presumed dangerous. Any information please call 1-800-555-0177. Recognizing the face, she immediately called the number. The authorities were at the West Motel within one hour and went directly to his room.

I arose from the bed, turned on Chopin's Funeral March by the London Philharmonic Orchestra with Nicholas Braithwaite conducting and Jack Gibbons, the guest soloist on piano on iTunes on my phone. I walked naked to the bathroom and set a warm bath. I then retrieved my laptop and started typing, adding to the manuscript of my current and last book. I looked at the page and began to type, the final paragraph. I opened my switch blade and proceeded to slowly cut my wrists, deep cuts that would bleed profusely enough so there was no turning back. I thought of the parallel and ironic justice that I was about to accomplish. I wondered how I would be judged within this context. As I was fading, feeling weaker and weaker, I heard the persistent and loud knocking on the door to the room and acknowledged the soon to be inevitable crash of the door being knocked down. Before I closed my eyes, I typed a note to Maria. Then I typed the title page of the book **"Confession"**…

EPILOGUE

"Confession," by Evan Dicks, annotated by Maria Lopez, a graduate of the Columbia School of Journalism, according to the biographical notes, became an international bestseller fueled by the morbid curiosity about the mind of a serial killer as evidenced by the popularity of shows like "Mindhunter" and "Dexter" and other true crime reality series. In addition, the unique first-person account of the psychology of the protagonist was consistent with this curiosity. Of note, the details of Evan Dicks psychology paralleled the work of Dr. Dorothy Otnow Lewis, who studied multiple serial killers and learned that many had abusive childhoods and dissociative identity disorders, previously called multiple personality disorders.

This allowed the serial killer to appear normal at times and yet able to commit horrific acts. The resemblance of the work of Dr. Dorothy Lewis with this serial killer psychology to Evan Dicks' first-person account made "Confession" a unique eyewitness account of this turmoil and thus piqued the public's interest. Interestingly, academics also found the book important, and it became an adjunct piece in the study of the criminal mind, especially that of a serial killer.

"Deadly Motivations" became a critically acclaimed and popular limited series on Netflix earning an Emmy award for adapted writing. Ironically, "Confession" was bought by Sony Pictures and turned into an award-winning film by Andrew Sorkin. Thus, Evan Dicks reviled for his criminal acts was indeed celebrated for his writing prowess. The legacy he spoke about was indeed realized.

Maria Lopez graduated from the Columbia University School of Journalism and went on to a successful career as a non-fiction author of biographies of great mathematical geniuses with emphasis on their works, with clear understandable concepts for the general public. The note that Evan had left asked her to make sure that "Confession" would be published and to help edit it. With the publication of "Confession," she was often asked about Evan Dicks, she remembered him as a brilliant writer with a troubled soul. She related that he seemed more open with her than anyone else, but she regretted that she couldn't help him more. She explained numerous times how fortunate she was to have known him in spite of his crimes.

Imani Moss was promoted to Executive Vice-President of Research and Development of Twitter's Artificial Intelligence division and has continued her consulting work with the FBI tracking violent crime suspects, thus enhancing Agent Joseph Esposito's profiling program and contributing to the remembrance of her good friend.

Capt. Ronald Captree, fully recovered, after many months of rehabilitation reconciled with Detective Alexandra Saunders. They currently reside in New York with his daughter, Claudia, and are both detectives in the Homicide Division of the 6th precinct. They enjoy a productive and serene life together. Claudia Captree currently attends Stuyvesant High School in Lower Manhattan. She maintains an excellent school record and is an accomplished pianist hoping to attend Julliard.

James Dicks lives in Boston with his aunt, Judith Baylor. He attends Austin Prep. He is an average student but is an outstanding running back on the football team and is being recruited by a number of Division 1 schools. He appears to be a well-adjusted teenager enjoying video games, carousing with friends, dating, attending parties and playing football. He has a steady girl fiend, who appropriately is the captain of the cheerleading team. James hardly ever talks about Evan but does think about him all the time. He thinks about the horrors that transpired with his parents that so affected his mind and psyche. He thinks about his belligerent father and seemingly loving mother and can't grasp the evil of them and the resultant damage to his brother. He occasionally cries and wishes it were all different, His aunt remembers her sister and her relationship with her two sons and how they turned out and the responsibility she bares. She does not have any difficulties with James and is very proud of his development. She always comments about his likable personality and his outgoing manner and appreciates his caring and devotion to his family and peers. He seems unaffected by what happened to his brother. His psyche seems to have not suffered by the evil that transpired in his early life. He never speaks about it or inquires about it. It all seems a distant memory without consequence. But…

www.markosia.com

www.ingramcontent.com/pod-product-compliance
Lightning Source LLC
Chambersburg PA
CBHW070850260626
47170CB00007B/2568